How to Steal a Submarine

Christopher P Clark

ISBN:
ISBN-13:9781731031082

DEDICATION

I dedicate this story to all submariners of every nation. Only we know real camaraderie.

By the same Author

HMS Hermes and the Virgin Sailor.

http://www.amazon.co.uk/HERMES-Virgin-Sailor-Christopher-Clark/dp/1516917790/ref=sr_1_1?ie=UTF8&qid=1454852656&sr=8-1&keywords=hms+hermes+and+the+virgin+sailor

CONTENTS

ACKNOWLEDGMENTS

I thank my wonderful wife for her support, encouragement and time, without which this work would still be just an idea.

I must also give thanks to my best friend, Indy Bhandal, for his 'Red Pen'.

I am forever grateful to the readers of my first story, HMS Hermes and the Virgin Sailor, who complimented me so much and encouraged me to write further. I hope you will not be disappointed.

I have a special thanks to my Facebook friend who introduced me to 'Z'. I have been trying to contact you. If you see this, please send me a message.

Chapter 1

A Mornings Walk

It was the summer of 1985 when Ian McTeil stepped over the threshold of his old stone cottage and surveyed the familiar and timeless scene. Although it was early, the summer's morning sun had already awakened the landscape. Ian was 86 years old and had lived in this cottage all his life. He was the only son of a mother who had suffered seven miscarriages. It was Ian's father's great grandfather who had built the house, from local materials, and subsequent sons had lived there. However, this tradition of habitation was due to end soon as there was no offspring to continue with this custom. Ian, and his wife Irene, had only one child, a son, who was determined not to spend his life in the same way as his fathers had done before him. The son left to join the British Army when he was seventeen years old. Two years later he was killed by the IRA, in Northern Ireland.

Ian's pale blue eyes surveyed the horizon. The sky was clear and there was no sign of rain. The sun was rising behind the house and he was yet to step out from the shade. He looked to the right at the wide expanse of beach. A crescent shaped splash of pale yellow reaching down to the dark grey North Atlantic. The Gulf Stream kept this part of Northern Scotland warm and beautiful; it was hidden from southerners who were unaware of its existence.

The salt air stung Ian's nostrils as he took his first deep breath. Seagulls swooped and soared and squawked throughout.

Ian's aging Border Collie dog - Rosie - pushed past him, almost buckling his knees as she squeezed through the narrow doorway, in her excitement to get out into the freedom of the outside world. Every morning Rosie exited the house with the same excitement and enthusiasm. She sniffed around, squatted and quickly squirted a jet of urine over some heather; not enough to empty her bladder as she would repeat this process several times during her spell of freedom from the house. Later she would sniff around more earnestly searching for a place to defecate, which would be some distance from the house, and there she would do her real business and the rest would be fun and frolics.

Other gulls romped in the indistinct line, where the sea lapped the shore, searching for breakfast amongst the flotsam brought in by the tide. They danced and hopped as if trying to prevent their feet getting wet. Ian could immediately see a strange bright orange object on the beach. This stirred a great deal of interest in him. He walked the beach every day and surveyed what the tide had left from the night before. He collected objects of interest and items of value. He scrutinised the driftwood and selected specific shapes, which he kept. He could see "forms" in these pieces of wood, which others could not. He would take them home and combine them with other pieces he had collected previously, and crude animals would be born. His house was surrounded by such sculptures giving the illusion of a surreal landscape and unnatural world. He also carried with him a large plastic bag, which he would fill with all the plastic debris - mainly empty bottles. Later he would give these bags to the mobile grocery delivery lady who would take them for recycling. Ian loved his beach.

Irene followed him out of the house although she could not walk as steadily as her husband. Irene was 86 years old also but suffered from arthritis – particularly in the knees and hips. However, she was determined to accompany her husband and pet Rosie. She would lag behind and Ian would meet her again on his return from the beach. Alas Irene's progress was getting less each day, which was consistent with her increased pains.

'It's a beautiful day Reenie' Ian called over his shoulder. He said this every day no matter what the weather was like.
Ian walked on with a keen interest in the bright orange object on the beach. Irene followed on behind.

As Ian approached the orange mass, he became more and more confused as to what it could be. Closer still it looked like a dummy - a doll of human proportions. He had never seen anything like this before. Rosie had already reached it and trampled on it; sitting on what would be the chest. Rosie sniffed it over, and then sat beside it. Ian closed in on it, and deduced it was something resembling a deflated Michelin man. However, it was not totally deflated as there was a mass supporting Rosie, who had now jumped back on top of it. He made out arms and legs, but the head was a domed extension of the body from between the shoulders - no neck; almost like an alien.

Ian could see that the material was rubberised, similar to suits which fishermen used in the twilight of his career. In his day protective clothing was black oilskins.

Ian slowed his approach as he neared the object. Now it looked like an orange space suit, like the space suits he had seen on television, many years before, when the men walked on the moon. The only piece that was not orange was where the face would be; this was plastic - clear transparent plastic.

Ian's heart began to race. He was frightened. He arrived and tentatively kicked my shoulder. He looked down at me, through the clear plastic facemask. Down at my lifeless wide eyes. His breath caught in his throat and his jaw dropped. It was as if his jaw was connected to his eyelids because they both simultaneously widened. He backed off, almost falling. 'Reenie!' he shouted. Then shouted again 'Reenie! We have a dead body here! Quick! Go back to the house and radio the Harbour master.'

Chapter 2

Recruitment

Alwyn Leonard sat on a bar stool with his shoulders hunched over his near empty pint glass which he cradled on both hands. The Two Trees in Plymouth was a favourite place to start his run ashore. There were few people in this bar around this time. Later it would fill up more and it would be too noisy and busy for Alwyn and he would move on.

Alwyn always liked to go ashore alone; he liked his own company. The truth was not too many people liked him though. Alwyn was a big man. He was over 6 foot and carried no fat. He was a powerful man who was ready to fight should he need to. In fact, sometimes he purposely went looking for trouble and a fight.

I liked Alwyn. We both served together on Submarine Valiant some time before. I couldn't take too much of him though. He tended to mumble, and it was difficult to comprehend him. His thick welsh accent didn't help matters either. On board we called him Lanky Leonard because he was lanky and always had to walk about the submarine with his head bowed else, he'd be bashing it against the pipes and fittings in the deck head. Some people called him Lurch as he seemed to 'lurch' around the boat. He did have a Frankenstein look about him; bulging bushy eyebrows and a big square jaw. His hands were huge and hung like weights on long arms which seemed to accentuate his lurch. All-in-all though, most women considered him to be a handsome man.

Lanky came from a family of miners and he was destined to follow suit until he joined the Navy. However, he always retained his opinion of governments being anti miners and anti trade unions. His family always lived in council houses and voted Labour at every general election. He was suspicious of businessmen as they gave an air of having wealth. He always thought they must be some sort of crooks to be so comfortably well off. He hated politicians even the Labour ones.

Alwyn was twice divorced. He had two children with his first wife, and together they were very young to start a family let alone get married. They sort of drifted apart and eventually his wife had had enough and filed for divorce. Lanky resented it, not because he didn't know it was over, but because he had to pay. His wife never worked - she couldn't with the two young kids - but the court ruled that Alwyn should provide for her. Alwyn had no choice; the court had made the decision and the Navy stopped the money out of his pay and handed it over to his ex-wife.

Lanky was pretty pissed off with this and did a runner. He went on leave and met some guy who was working on the construction of the M1 motorway. The work was hard, but the guy was earning a shit-load of money. He said he could get Lanky a job so Lanky didn't come back from leave. Everything was not that simple though. After a while he got fed up with the long hours, in all weathers, and the backbreaking work finally wore him down. Not only that he had to share a house with a load of other guys whom he didn't get along with too well. He finally turned himself in to a recruiting office and, after a period of punishment, resumed his Naval career.

His athletic stance and chiseled good looks soon turned the head of an out of work actress. He fell for her big time, she was beautiful, and they were soon married. When she worked things were good, but she spent a lot of time 'between positions'. She soon became pregnant and couldn't work. Money was tight as Lanky was still paying for his first wife and kids – which he never got to see. One day he arrived home for the weekend un-expected and found her in their bed with another man. Lanky was furious but just turned away and left the house. Lanky must have known that should he lose his temper with the guy, he may end up killing him. He also knew his wife was more to blame and could easily kill her also. His wife filed for divorce and Lanky Leonard had to pay again. The courts said so, and the Navy stopped his pay and gave the money to her; same as before.

Poor Lanky had next to no money each month. He had no car and no house. He had no money to go away at the weekends and even if he did, he had nowhere to go. He would sit in the corner of the Two Trees depressing himself in a depressing place.

On this particular occasion, an equally tall guy entered the Two Trees and approached the bar next to Lanky. This man wore smart grey slacks with a green tweed jacket. He had a crispy clean shirt with a smart silk tie. Lanky, whose eyes were normally down cast, noticed his brown brogue shoes were highly polished. He glanced up at the man, taking in his blond hair and thick black-rimmed glasses and thought he looked like Joe 90. The man caught his eye and nodded to him. Lanky grunted and turned his attention back to his near empty pint glass.

The man took out his wallet, rested his hands on the bar and waited to be noticed by the bar staff. A girl sauntered over and raised her head in an inquiring manner. ‘A pint of your best bitter please’ said the man politely.

Lanky thought he was some kind toff and took an instant dislike to him. ‘Would you like to join me with a beer?’ the man asked Alwyn.

Lanky was taken aback and looked up at the man ‘That would be nice’ he replied and then drained his glass and pushed it towards the bargirl.

Lanky thought his luck had changed. He was getting a free beer. Lanky had no intention of buying the guy a beer in return - lanky never did that; he couldn’t afford it.

The man pulled up a stool, and as he sat down, he sniffed the air; ‘Always smell this bad in here’ he asked, ‘I guess it’s the carpet is it?’

Again, Lanky nodded a grunt in reply. The beer came and Lanky said his thanks to the man.

The two began a conversation and Alwyn gained a liking for the man particularly when he bought him a second beer. The man introduced himself as John Smith. Alwyn thought this was funny as that's the name you give when you don't want to give your real name. However, someone must have that name for real he supposed.

After some time, when John had ordered a third beer for Alwyn, Alwyn apologised for not buying a beer by saying he had no money. 'No problem at all.' reassured John 'I got plenty of money and am happy to chat with you. You are an interesting guy and I like your views on trade unions.'

Lanky wondered if John was some sort of queer but suspected not. In any case Lanky knew that if the guy laid a hand on him, he'd be knocked into the middle of next week.

Lanky met John twice again, in the Two Trees, during that week. They had not arranged to meet but again John was happy to buy Lanky beer and Lanky was happy to receive it.

The two met several more times during the following days and weeks. John always turned the conversation around to the trade unions, left-ish politics and the divide in wealth between rich and poor let alone the injustices of the divorce system, where the woman seemed always to win and could go back to the courts for more money when inflation devalued what she received. John noted how Alwyn would talk with such bitterness on these subjects.

'Alwyn' John asked, 'what would you do if someone gave you a million pounds?'

Lanky looked at him and grunted. He turned his attention to his beer and grunted again. 'A million quid eh' he paused, and John intently waited for him to reply, 'I'd have to give it to the bitches so what's the fucking point.'

'No no.' reassured John. 'What if you had a million pounds and you could just disappear with it,' John waited for a reaction 'where no-one could find you,' another pause 'ever!' John concluded.

Lanky huffed and grunted again. 'Well that would be good' he looked at John 'but it could never happen.'

'Look Alwyn' John said earnestly 'What would you "do" for a million pounds?'

Lanky looked at him directly. Joe 90's face looked straight back at him without expression except for the slight rise of his right eyebrow inviting a response. Lanky could see no sign of jesting. He turned back to his beer and matter-of-factly said 'Well, I guess I'd do just about anything.'

John nodded at his reply. Now it was John who turned his attention back to his beer. Without looking at Alwyn he asked, 'And what would you "do" with one million pounds Alwyn?' Alwyn was silent. Now with a smile on his face and some joviality in his voice 'Give it some though. I'd be interested to know what you would do.'

Alwyn did not go into the Two Trees for a few days but not because he was avoiding John. He had to admit to himself he was a little disturbed by what John had said yet he was intrigued to know what he would say when they met again. Also, he had daydreamed about the prospect of having a million quid. He'd buy a boat and sail around the world.

'I'd buy a boat and sail around the world' Alwyn told John when he had placed a pint of Guinness in front of him when they met the next time.

'Ah!' said John 'That's a good idea. Money well spent and gets you away. You could disappear easily and wouldn't have to give the 'bitches' anything.' He emphasised the word bitches because Alwyn had used that word.

This theme continued, and John steered the conversation into what type of boat and that, with a million pounds, he could get one built to his own specification. He even informed Alwyn there were great boat builders in Poole Dorset, further implanting the seed of thought.

Finally, John asked again 'So, what would you "do" to get one million pounds?' Now more surely, Alwyn answered

'I'd do anything.'

'Anything?'

'Anything.'

'Would you kill?' Alwyn was surprised at the way the conversation was going 'Would you kill for one million pounds?' John said again and before Alwyn replied 'Assuming you would get away with it. No-one would know and then you would get your boat and be off.'

'For fuck sake John what's the fucking point of talking like this. You do my fucking head in.' John could see Alwyn was getting agitated.

'Well, if you could betray your country and, in the process, people die - not women or children - then I could give you one million pounds.'

Alwyn looked at John with horror. John continued 'You would not have to kill anyone directly just be part of one act of betrayal. If you could agree to that then I would give you one million pounds and I would give you a second million pounds when the deed is done.'

'Fucking hell John. What the fuck would I have to do?'

'One act of national betrayal. Some people will die. Some may be your friends and that's it. You would never be in danger and you won't be alone. You can consider it as you being part of a catastrophe. You will survive, and others will survive, but no-one will know. You will be considered as one of the victims and so no-one would be looking for you.'

Alwyn thought. He hated having no money. He had no car. No prospect of ever buying a car. Without the Navy he had nowhere to live. One act of betrayal. Treason. *'So, what'* he thought. *People die all the time and I don't give a shit. Shit happens. People will always die.* 'If I say yes what happens next?'

'Well, think about it. If you say yes, I will arrange a transfer of one million pounds to an offshore account and you will have the access numbers. You can begin to spend the money however you want. In a few weeks you will be invited to a meeting, along with more people like you, where details of what is expected of you will be revealed. If you don't like it, then just give me the money back and you can carry on as you are.'

'Well, sounds simple enough.' Alwyn intoned submissively.

'It is simple. Give me your answer next time we meet.' Alwyn nodded his understanding. 'Surely I don't need to warn you that these conversations are strictly private between us. It will do you no good to repeat anything to anyone else.' Alwyn looked through the lenses of the Joe 90 glasses and felt a chill crawl up his back. He realised the man was serious and, for the first time dangerous.

On the evenings when John Smith was not with Alwyn Leonard in the Two Trees he was with other people in the local haunts of Plymouth and other places. One of the guys he had targeted was Jock Thames. I had served with Jock many years ago on the Hermes; we were both juniors together although I was a year older than he. Jock was a bull-shitter and quite good at it too. In those early days he convinced us all he had GCE 'A' levels and was being considered for helicopter pilot training. His girlfriend gave the impression she came from a family of considerable wealth. This too was bullshit. The two married very early in life. Jock was only 17 and she a year older. She was pregnant. After the Hermes I kept in touch with Jock from time to time. I was climbing the ladder of promotion, but he was not. He was getting fat and drinking far too much. He had a large round face with staring blue eyes. His speech was always a bit slurred; it always was, and spittle would accumulate at the corner of his mouth. Despite this I liked Jock and we got together as often as we could. The last time I saw him, three or four years before, was in Plymouth when I had just qualified as a Nuclear Chief of the Watch on submarines. Jock was still looking up at the first rung on the ladder of promotion. Jock, at that time had not joined the submarine service.

Jock now sat on a stool at a bar in one of the pubs in the Barbican of Plymouth. Two hands cupped his pint glass and there was a wry smile on his face and a glazed expression in his eyes. 'If you gave me one million pounds, I would buy a house on the Costa del Sol of Spain and play golf every day.' he said to Mr. John Smith. 'There is an unbelievable amount of golf courses there and many more will be created in the coming years.' John looked at him and nodded his head slowly. He allowed Jock to continue. 'I would buy a big house, with a view of the Mediterranean and it would have a swimming pool. I would play golf in the morning, at a different course each day, and get pissed by the pool in the afternoon.'

John knew that Jock had money problems; Jock always had money problems. Jock never had any money except that which he borrowed with no prospect of paying back. He would pay his debt by staying on board doing a weekend duty for someone who could then get home. Jock had told John of his love of golf and how he considered it to be the ultimate sport. Just one man and a silly white ball against everything. Jock could play the game but, like most amateurs, lacked consistency. At times he could hit a ball as far as he had seen professional hit one on the TV. He had beaten par on holes as he had seen the same professionals do on television. Most amateur golfers can do the same. However, what they cannot do is do it consistently. They cannot do it hole after hole. If one should birdie one hole the feeling of euphoria is great, and it instils a feeling of such confidence that finally you think you have 'arrived'. Now you can approach the next hole with confidence and bravado. A couple of practice swings and you feel good. This next ball will sail down the fairway like nobody's business. Then you bend down and put that little round ball on its tee - ready to be launched away. Next you address the ball; place the club head behind it - doubt begins to creep in. You dismiss the doubt. You have just birdied the previous hole and have reached a mile-stone in the game of golf. You are knocking on the door of the professionals. You look down at the ball. You flex your thigh muscles and tighten your fingers on one another as you might rub your hands prior to selecting your favourite cup cake from a tray. The club doesn't feel right but you dismiss it. You start the back swing and stare down hard at the ball - keeping your head still. At the top of the back swing the thighs tighten once again; a slight pause; and the explosive swing begins. Your lips have tightened, and breath is held. You are determined to punish this little mother-fucking, cock-sucking, shit of a white ball. Thwack! Then you are in the follow through. You've duffed the shot! The ball scuttles away, instead of flying high in the sky, and you are brought back to earth. A quick look around to see if anyone was looking and then march off. Fuck! Fuck! Fuck! Goes through your mind in frustration, anger and embarrassment.

Jock knew for sure what he would do with one million quid.

Jock also was a loner. He lived with the junior rates, but he was 10 to 15 years older than them, so they all shared very different views to his. Their taste in music differed and their general behaviour was different - more childish Jock considered. Jock continued to bullshit, and all his messmates knew of it. He was not a very popular person.

When John proposed giving Jock one million pounds with another one million to follow Jock agreed immediately. He was told that he must commit one act of treason, along with some others, and people would die. When John offered, that Jock, could consider himself as being involved in a catastrophe, which he survived although the general public would think he was also a victim and had been one of the many that were not recovered, it was an easy decision for Jock to make. After the event he would be playing Golf in the South of Spain.

John said goodbye to Jock but promised to see him soon with details of the first million pounds and a to let him know when the meeting would be held to outline the requirements of him.

During the next few weeks John gave away £8,000,000. Apart from a golfer and a global sailor he financed a would-be Dinosaur hunter; Gold prospector; Amazon explorer; Caribbean sunken treasure hunter; one was sure that he was privy to certain information which would lead him to the Holy grail, and the last was going to buy a mobile home and convert it to all terrain use and drive around the World at his leisure.

John reported to his superiors he was ready to move onto the next stage of the project.

Chapter 3

The Briefing

Alwyn Leonard and Jock Thames both received a letter from Mr John Smith on the same day. The letter instructed them to attend a Personnel Vetting meeting at the Union Jack Club (UJC) in Waterloo London, in two days' time. They were both informed that their Divisional Officers had been notified of this meeting. The letter was written on official Ministry of Defense (Royal Navy) headed paper and signed by Mr. John Smith with a title of Head of Submarine Personnel Security. They were instructed to report to the reception, at the UJC, and would be shown where the meeting would be held. They were informed that a total of eight people would be attending the meeting and they were not to speak with the other attendees except for the courtesy of normal greetings. A return rail ticket to London was also included.

Alwyn looked at the signature hard and wondered if this was the same Mr John Smith as he had met some weeks before. Was this a set-up. Had he been tricked into agreeing something and now he would be dragged over the coals for it. Panic set in. If that were the case, why would they give him one million pounds Sterling.

Someone had given him one million pounds Sterling it was a fact. He was given details of the account with an account number, which identified him as the account holder. He was advised to change the number so only he would know it and then no one else would be able to access his account. If he wanted, he could transfer the money to any account anywhere in the world. He changed his number and had access to the money. He had even spent some of it. In fact, he had spent a great deal of it.

Alwyn had approached a boat builder in Poole Harbour and discussed his requirement. He didn't really know what he wanted and so entered into a long discussion with the company and together they came up with a solution. A standard design could be modified and built with those modifications to satisfy Alwyn's needs. Alwyn needed a sailboat large enough to cope with all seas around the world. He needed it to be equipped with sufficient power-mechanised equipment, so he could sail it single-handed. He needed the latest; most sophisticated yet most user-friendly radar, radio and navigation equipment. It also needed a fairly large inboard motor and independent generator.

All his requirements were met. He gave the boat builders an assumed name in which the boat should be registered, as he didn't want any comeback to himself. He gave an address of 'no fixed abode'. The boat builders required Identity but he had none in his assumed name. He had to give a unique code number to identify him. The builders also needed payment. They came up with a contract, which required stage payments as the build progressed and Alwyn signed it and provided the authorisation for his bank to make the payments. Everyone was happy, and building commenced.

As confused as Alwyn was, he had no option but to attend the meeting. The next couple of days were excruciating. He was full of anxiety and indeed he was scared stiff that he would be in big trouble. He boarded a train at Plymouth bound for London. He stood outside the UJC and was relieved, in some way, that he would find out his fate fairly soon now. He was early so went into the Wellington pub next door. He ordered a pint of Guinness and a double Wood's rum.

Jock Thames cautiously opened the letter. He knew it was official by the initials OHMS on the envelope and the quality of the paper used to make it. It seemed a very official letter telling him to attend a Personnel Vetting meeting. He had joined the Submarine service only a couple of years previous and he'd heard of other people having to attend such an interview. Jock knew he was a bit of a bull-shitter but never considered this should constitute a security risk. He then began to panic wondering if this had anything to do with the series of conversations with Mr John Smith. He had confirmed to Mr John Smith that he would be willing to commit an act of treason, where several people would die, in return for a total of two million pounds. He knew now it would be no good denying it as he had already received a one-million-pound payment! He was given details of the account and changed the account number to one of his own creation. He had placed a large deposit with a construction company building luxury villas on one of the most prestigious golf courses on the Costa del Sol in Spain. He did not know if anyone else knew of his newfound fortune. He had said nothing to no-one and he had not splashed his money about except for the proposed move to Spain. He had looked at watches; he always wanted a good watch. He always wanted a beautiful expensive watch. He was looking at Cartier and Rolex but the most beautiful so far was Piaget.

Jock looked at the train ticket and felt he had no option but to attend. He decided he would just check in with his Divisional Officer to make sure he did know, and to find out if he knew why he would have to attend such a meeting. Then, when he was about to put the paperwork away, he noticed the signature, Mr John Smith! He accepted this was one of the most common names in Great Britain but had a feeling this was not just a coincidence. Could it really be the same person? This Mr John Smith was Head of Submarine Personnel Security. Jock accepted he was waiting to be contacted again but was this really it? Jock too, like Alwyn considered he had been tricked into saying something he would now regret. If that was the case, why the million quid? If he was being tricked into saying something, they didn't need to give him the money - the deed had already been done.

Un-be-known to each other Jock and Alwyn had traveled to London on the same train. They had traveled across London independently and both arrived early at the UJC. Jock also went into the Wellington and ordered a pint. Jock was first to leave. Alwyn followed a few minutes later. Alwyn was a Nuclear Chief of the Watch and had a fantastic sense of timing. Jock would leave a greater margin of error. Alwyn was the last to enter the meeting room.

A table had been prepared with seating for eight - four on either side. Alwyn took the remaining seat whilst nodding around at the already seated attendees. Everyone seemed embarrassed and kept their eyes lowered to the table top; their hands in their laps. Alwyn's timing was exact. Almost immediately another door opened and in walked Mr John Smith. There seemed to be a general feeling of relief as they all recognised Mr John Smith as the one they had a series of conversations with some few weeks before. This tall, well groomed, gentleman took a position at the head of the table. He scanned his recruits through his thick rimmed glasses with an inscrutable face. Then his face cracked into a smile and he greeted the assembly with a warm 'Hello. Thank you all for coming.' There was a pause, more for effect than anything else and then John continued. 'You people have been carefully selected for the special things you know and your own very special circumstances. You people share more in common than you would generally believe. You are special people. Special to the needs of the people who have engaged me to recruit you. I too share things in common with you.' and as he said 'you' his hands spread out in front of him embracing the whole gathering. 'I will cut to the chase. I have had numerous conversations with you all and offered you one million pounds if you would be willing to commit one act of high treason - one act of country betrayal where a number of people will die - some may be your friends.' There was a pause as John looked around the table and the gathering began to lift up their heads and looked around warily at each other although still nervous and embarrassed. 'One million pounds will follow once my task is complete. You have all agreed to this and you have all received the first payment. In fact, you have all accessed the money and committed substantial amounts into your planned disappearances after the event.

'Gentlemen, you should know that I too will commit the same act of treason and bear witness to men dying. I am currently employed by the Ministry of Defence but, I too have been recruited with a brief to recruit you' and again his arms went out as a form of embrace 'to assist me in this. I too have received a payment and will receive more on completion.'

Alwyn, Jock and the rest inwardly relaxed some although there was still a long way to go before everything would be explained.

'Please Gentlemen I would ask you to introduce yourselves to each other. Please stand up in turn say you name age and position. If you would start,' he pointed to Alwyn 'and then we will go around from the left.'

Alwyn stood up. 'My name is Alwyn Leonard. I am 35 years old. I am a Chief Petty officer and Nuclear Chief of the Watch on Nuclear Submarines.' He then sat down.

'Hello, I am Brian Wilson, they call me Tug. I am 35 years old, a Chief Petty Officer a Mechanical Chief of the Watch, forward systems, on Nuclear submarines.'

The next rose to his feet just as Tug sat down 'My name is Rees Jennings. I am a chef. Well, cook really. I am 27 years old. I am also a submariner.'

Some of the people sniggered at the correction of cook from chef. Jock stood up 'Hi I am Raymond Thames, but they call me Jock because I'm Scottish.' It was clear from his accent he was Scottish. 'I am 36 years old and am an electrical rating working on forward systems of a Submarine.' he concluded and then wondered if he should say he was still a junior rate. He opted to sit down instead.

A small ginger haired figure stood up next. His skin was pale and contrasted against the shock of red hair on his head. His goofy teeth were a prominent feature of his face. His skin was clear, and it looked as if he had never shaved in his life. 'I am Joe Green. I am an expert in sonar systems.' the man spoke with a thick accent advertising the fact he was from Norfolk. 'I have contributed to investigations of marine incidents, particularly submarines, by analysing sonar recordings. I am 38 years old and been a Chief Petty Officer in the Submarine service for 8 years.' almost as an afterthought he added 'They call me Ginge.'

Thomas Gill rose slowly. He stood with his shoulders back and his head cocked forward in an arrogant stance. He was tall with an athletic build. He looked around the table with the faintest of smiles dancing around his mouth. His eyes were steely. 'I am Thomas Gill - Gilly' he paused a little. I am a Killick stoker but used to be a Petty Officer. I got busted for going walk-about.' He paused again. 'Should get my rate back in about six months - if I'm good.' He paused and watch peoples' reaction. He had their attention. 'I've been in boats nearly 15 years. I am 35 years old and work on forward mechanical systems.

'Dennis Warr' Dennis announced as he was rising. 'CPO. Back aft artificer. 33' then he sat back down.

Finally, Paul Wells stood and introduced himself. 'They call me Bomber. I am a tiff 2 but get my buttons soon (This meant he was a second-class Artificer and Petty Officer. Buttons on the uniform sleeve signify a Chief Petty Officer so he was expecting this promotion soon). 'I am electrical trained and assist the

Mechanical Chief of the Watch on fwd. systems. I am 26.'

'Gentlemen, thank you for that' John said when all were seated again before him.

Mr John Smith paused to investigate the faces of his gathering. He could see them more relaxed and comfortable now. He deliberately prolonged the pause and he knew that each one of his recruits were desperate to be told what they needed to do. 'In the last few days you will have all received notification that you are to join Her Majesty's Submarine Messenger.' His eyebrows raised as if to invite a response. Each person nodded, some muttered agreement and they looked around some at the newly-to-be shipmates.

'Our special mission is to steal that Submarine.' John announced solemnly.

All eyes now fixed on John. Some jaws dropped. No-one could believe what they were hearing. No-one had ever stolen a submarine!

'We will incapacitate the entire crew and take charge ourselves. We will rendezvous with a courier who will take the submarine from us, and our job will be done.' John raised his eyebrows again, hunched his shoulder and outstretched is arms with palms facing upwards - a classic gesture of saying 'easy'.

There followed a long pause and John knew the turmoil that would be going through their minds. John continued 'The courier would be in the form of a specially designed super-tanker. We will manoeuvre ourselves beneath it and surface into it. The inside is equipped with a mooring jetty with all the normal shore-side services we would need. Hydraulic doors would close the ship's hull and it would then sail away as normal. We connect shore supplies and shut down the reactor. Our job will then be complete. We will be landed ashore by helicopter.' John looked around and saw the incredulity on the faces of his recruits. Each had a ton of questions, but none aired them at this moment.

'However,' John continued raising his finger as he spoke 'you may be required, at a later date, to give training to the new crew. If so, you will be paid handsomely for this extra service.'

John had explained - briefly - how the Submarine would be dealt with once control had been attained but he had not explained how the crew would be 'incapacitated.' John knew that each of his special eight were mulling this around in their minds. The eight attendees began to look around at each other trying to read each other's' thoughts.

Alwyn knew that to incapacitate the crew would mean killing them. That's why John had cautioned that 'some would die'. The thought horrified him. He, and the ones around the table, had to kill the entire crew of the Submarine. Alwyn had doubts of whether he would be able to do this.

It was Jock Thames who croaked 'Sir?' as he raised his arm with finger pointing to the ceiling. His eyes were staring wide as he looked at John. 'How do we incapacitate the crew?'

The rest of John's eight were relieved Jock had broken the ice and asked the question. All eyes now turned to Mr John Smith who looked around with no expression on his face. In a solemn voice he confirmed their worst fear. 'They will all die, and we will dispose of them'. Alwyn's heart skipped a beat. Tug involuntarily gasped and Rees the chef/cook dropped his head into his hands. Others were able to contain their thoughts and emotions. John allowed this information to sink in as he studied his chosen few.

'However.' John said holding his hand up as if to calm them all. 'You will not have to kill anyone personally. I will take care of that.'

'How?' asked Rees.

'You don't need to know that at this stage.' said John with authority. 'You all knew, in the beginning, that people would die. You all accepted this, and you all took the money.' John paused. 'It is too late to turn back now. Even if you returned the money, and none of you can, the powerful people who have engaged me would not like the idea that someone knows of our plans.' The veiled threat did not need to be expanded upon.

Alwyn quickly assessed the situation. He thought of his boat nearing build completion in Poole and the prospect of getting away from all his problems. It is true he knew people would die and he is somewhat relieved to learn he would not have to kill them himself although he accepted he would share a responsibility in their deaths.

Mr John Smith cautioned his crew about talking about their plans. He even advised they should not socialise with each other. He would deliver further instructions as a when they were necessary.

'How do we know we will not be ***incapacitated*** once we deliver the Submarine?' Tug asked the question that was on everyone's mind.

'Good question.' John anticipated this question. 'I suggest you keep a record of all this information including the bank details especially the initial deposit. Lodge it with a solicitor or bank manager in a sealed envelope only to be opened in the event of an unexplained death. Governments are involved, and the initial deposits of money can be traced using such high authority. Therefore, it would be in the interest of our benefactors to keep you all alive.'

This explanation reassured the attendees somewhat and the stiffness went out of the gathering.

John explained that he would be on Submarine Messenger when they joined and be able to keep them all informed of events and requirements. Further details of the plan would be fed into them. John did not invite any further questions and announce the meeting was over and wished everyone a safe journey.

Alwyn strolled back into the Wellington closely followed by Tug Brian Wilson. They stood elbow to elbow at the bar each expecting the other to order. A skinny girl came in a very short dress. She had no tits and her skinny legs didn't merit ogling, so Tug looked into her face. He instantly wished he didn't - she was ugly with crooked teeth too big for her mouth. Conceding Tug ordered a Pint of Guinness and ask Alwyn what he wanted. 'Same' Alwyn said, with a feeling of triumph, then added 'thanks.' Alwyn turned away from the bar to find a table and Tug checked the arse under the girl's short dress - he could see no defined swelling beneath the material and so turned away.

'What do you reckon to that then.' Tug asked. Alwyn really didn't want to speak to him so just grunted. They both felt awkward. Tug wanted to talk, and Alwyn didn't. Brian Wilson and Alwyn Leonard will be the most senior people of Mr John Smiths recruited crew 'Do you think we can really pull this off?' Tug asked and was looking into Alwyn's face for a response. Tug was a big man. Easily as tall as Alwyn but broader and with more evidence of his beer drinking history. He had a mop of dark curly hair although his hairline was receding. Big bushy eyebrows hung over his small dark eyes. Tug's nose seemed to have a small ball at the end. He had a wiry, scraggy beard that made him look somewhat unkempt.

Alwyn did not look at him. He stared into his beer. Alwyn was still upset learning he would be part of killing a complete crew of a submarine - well almost a complete crew. 'I guess we'll fucking have to.'

'Do you think they'll kill us as well afterwards.' Tug probed.

Alwyn hunched is shoulders 'I don't fucking know. I don't even know if I wish I never met that Mr John fucking Smith. To me it's a solution to a fucked-up life. It could be a good way out but to be bumped off at the end is not too far away from where I am now.'

Tug digested this, and concluded Alwyn was in a state of depression. 'I suppose you, like me, are divorced. The missus has the kids and takes all your money.' Tug investigated Alwyn's face, but Alwyn's attention was fixed on his beer. 'Right?' Tug was pressing for an answer.

'And the fucking house.' Alwyn responded.

'I think all of us in that room have the same problem so to be tempted by a million quid is an easy solution.'

'Yeah' Alwyn conceded. 'Doesn't seem so fucking attractive now though.'

'Well look mate. We really don't have a choice now. We knew, we took the money now we must deliver.' Alwyn's face never moved, and his eyes remained fixed on his beer glass. 'So, what do you know about the Messenger then?' Tug asked changing the subject some.

Lanky Leonard seemed to snap out of his trance and looked up and took a sneaky peek into Tug's face. He couldn't meet his eyes though. 'It's new, small, fast, quiet has special torpedoes on board and three ballistic missiles. Oh, and it's the sneaky boat - long patrols.'

'Yeah and its pretty automated too so I hear.' Tug added 'and we get more dosh.'

Tug tried hard at conversation but to no avail. He considered Alwyn to be a miserable fucker. Alwyn told Tug he had to rush to get his train, which was a lie, he just didn't want to buy the man a beer in return. He got up and left grunting a good bye as he did so.

Chapter 4

A Morning in Faslane.

I opened my eyes and struggled to focus them on the ceiling of my cabin. I waited for my brain to tell me my head hurt through drinking too much whisky the night before. I always drank too much whisky the night before and my head always hurt in the mornings.

I was in the shore barracks of HMS Neptune on the Gare Loch just off the Clyde estuary. It was home to the largest UK Submarine squadron. I had joined Submarine Messenger some short time ago during the completion phase of its build in Philadelphia. I was part of a skeleton crew which had sailed the submarine from there to Faslane in readiness for full acceptance and sea trials. Faslane was the acknowledged name for the Submarine base. I had occupied such accommodation, in Faslane, off and on for 15 years since I had joined the Submarine service. We were not allowed to remain on the submarine overnight unless you were duty watch - everyone had an inboard cabin.

I sat up and swung my feet to the floor bracing myself, with my arms, against the edge of my bed. A wave of nausea and dizziness swept over me but passed quickly. I stood up, steadied myself, then moved to the window. I opened the curtains and looked out. It was raining. It mostly rained here. It was summer time and had been light for some time now. I didn't need to set any alarm. It was built into my brain that at 07:00 I would be awake.

It was a misty light that greeted me. I recalled, as I always did on such occasions, since receiving my first draft to a Submarine. I was on Submarine basic training course at HMS Dolphin, in Gosport and HMS/M Resolution is what it said on the draft chit – a Polaris Submarine. I was disappointed. I wanted a conventional diesel-powered boat based in Gosport, but you rarely got what you wanted in this Navy.

Accompanying the draft chit was a small leaflet of propaganda giving information about HMS Neptune, Helensburgh (the local town) and the general area. I always remember one line – '**The Gare Loch is renowned for it's beautiful scenery and rainy days. It is said that if you cannot see the other side of the Gare Loch it's because it is raining. However, if you can see the other side of the Gare Loch then it is just about to rain**' - nothing was truer.

I lifted the window, reached out and retrieved a can of McEwans ale. I had no fridge in my cabin so kept a couple of cans on the outside window-sill to keep cool. I ruptured the top with an opener making two triangular holes - one to let the beer out and the other to let the air in. I drank half of its contents in one go. I had to do this every morning before I did anything else. It was the only thing that kick-started my systems into gear. I sat down again on the bed and let the fluid settle my stomach and the effects of the alcohol chase away the pain in my head. Soon a feeling of euphoria swept over me and I was 'awake'. I went for a shower. I then got dressed, finished the rest of the beer and brushed my teeth. I checked my hip flask but, alas, it was empty. I stuffed it into my back pocket and left the cabin.

I made my way, through the drizzling rain to the Senior Rates dining room. Breakfast, for me, was always the same: two rashers of bacon, one fried egg, baked beans, one sausage and one piece of toasted bread. I never ate it all. The egg yoke, if it was soft, I would mop up with some toast. I shovelled a couple of forks-full of beans into my mouth and I selected some bits of the bacon - the bits that weren't too greasy. I always tasted the sausage but rarely ate it; it would be too fatty.

''ello Clarkie you ole fucker.' Chief Petty Officer Baldwin greeted me in a cheerful voice. Some-what surprised I looked up.

'Hello Bonker. How the fuck are you?' His name was Barry, but he got the name Bonker because he was always shagging someone. 'What ya doing? I aint seen you for ages.'

'Joining Messenger. I hear you are on her as well.'

'Yeah, just got here from Philli (Philadelphia). Great run ashore.' I confirmed.

'Sneaky boat I hear, with long trips away.'

'That's right,' I confirmed again 'but a shit-load more money as well.'

'Yeah, that's why I wanted it.' He said resignedly 'Not for the long trips mind you but the dosh.' he was quick to point out. Submarine Messenger was a brand-new Submarine specially designed to penetrate enemy waters and spy on enemy shipping and their submarine latest developments. It was considered a more arduous, and potentially dangerous draft, and so a supplement to the 'Submarine Pay' was awarded.

Bonker pulled up a chair, placed his plate on the table and joined me for breakfast. His plate was similarly populated as mine. He was younger than I and was in the tail end of a divorce. He would get very depressed about this from time to time. Relations with his wife were not good; she was taking him to court for sole custody of their children and to take possession of the house - Barry would have to continue paying the mortgage though. He loved his kids and would be reduced to tears whilst speaking to them on the telephone. However, he was a strong character and would soon get over these lapses of depression. He had an infectious laugh and would always chuckle at his own jokes inviting other people to follow. People did laugh with him but not at his jokes. It was his mannerisms which made people laugh.

He arrived at Faslane in a beautiful Mk10 Jaguar. This type of car had not been made for a few years and generally they turned into rust buckets. It had a massive 4.2 litre engine and triple carburetors. The Mk 10 jag was the biggest ever saloon car made in Britain. How on earth Barry could afford such a car, was a complete mystery to most people, especially when he was so far in the throws of divorce.

However, Barry confided in me that the car was given to him by some woman he had been shagging in Helensburgh. The woman lived in one of the mansions in the upper reaches of the town. He didn't know if she was divorced or not. It was clear the husband was not around. Barry didn't ask too many questions. The woman liked to be 'serviced' and Barry obliged. She was very happy, and she knew that Barry was short of cash, so she gave him a credit card which he could use to gas the car up when ever it needed it. Barry, up until now, had been serving at Rosyth - the other side of Scotland and the lady liked to see him on a regular basis so by giving him the car, and the credit card, Barry had no excuse.

'Golden bollocks.' I said with real envy. Everyone would love a woman like that. However, I'm sure there must be a catch somewhere along the line.

'She's a Yank.' Bonker told me. Met a rich Brit, they married, and he brought her here.

'So, what happened?' I asked.

'Well,' he said 'they got into a bit of wife swapping. Apparently, they had a few couples they would get together with and have a sort of mini orgy. It seems the man got a bit too fond of the other's wife and decided he wanted to jump ship. The other man pissed off, so her husband moved in with the woman in her house in Glasgow.'

'And you took his place at home.' I added 'Nice one.' I continued 'I don't suppose she's into swapping anymore then.'

'No, she's a bit possessive. She is a bit kinky though. Hardly ever gets dressed.'

'Really?' I responded with growing interest.

'Sometimes, when we go out, she just puts on a coat. Bollicky buff underneath.'

'Really!' I said again with more interest. 'She ever been to a cocktail party down a boat?' We both laughed at this remark.

'Who are you shagging these days then?'

'Well, I got some grommit in tow from Clydebank.' I told him.

'Well go on then.' he wanted to know more.

'Well, I met her at one of the dance parties they have in the senior rates mess from time to time. She's about ten years older than me and loves the jolly old thing. She'd come and collect me and take me back to her place for the evening, but we would stop off at some bars on the way.' Bonker listened attentively. 'She's the spitting image of Shirley Bassey; tall, thin, black hair, full lips and big dark eyes. I don't know if she could sing or not.' Bonker sniggered at that 'I call her SB, for obvious reasons, but she's called Sally. She lends me her car now and again.' I emphasised the word *lend* 'The idea was that when I left her, if she lent me her car, she knew I could return in a day or two. She also knew I had no spare cash. She don't know I lost my license though. Got caught driving over the limit.'

'Got done for drinking an' driving then Chris?' Bonker asked with real sympathy.

'Yeah. £200 fine and 12 months ban and then got done by the Navy for disgracing the Naval uniform.'

'Fuck me. Pusser (anything Navy) makes you go to court in rig then fucks you for doing so.'

'Well, as they say, Life in a Blue Suit.' We sat and pushed our food around the plate selecting pieces to eat.

'So, tell me more about this SB then Clarkie.'

'Not much to say really. She has a daughter who is absolutely beautiful - bit of a slag though I think.' Barry looked up from his breakfast and chewing his food he said.

'Why you say that?'

'Well, she wears a lot of make-up; too much really and tight jumpers, short skirts and high-heeled boots.'

'Sounds okay to me.' he mumbled as he turned his attention back to his plate.

'Yeah, it's okay but you wouldn't want your own daughter to go out like that.'

Barry nodded. 'Anyway, SB seems to be an older version of her daughter. She likes to wear sexy knickers cos she knows I like that. Sometimes she goes out with none on which is okay and sometimes she goes out with no bra on and, to be honest that's a mistake. She has saggy tits and they flop around a lot when they are free under some not-so-tight jumper.'

'Ha ha.' Barry chuckled 'Sounds okay. The best thing is she seems to like the jolly ole thing.'

'Yes sir. She does.'

'We'll have to get together sometime. The four of us. Could be a good night out.' Barry was looking at me again.

'I don't think SB is into swapping.'

'No no!' Barry was quick to add 'Nor is the Yank anymore. She's more into exhibition and voyeurism. She told me I can't fuck anyone else. Said she has learnt her lesson.'

The thought of us two in the presence of two old biddies flashing their bits in some bar seemed an enjoyable pastime which I would give more thought to in the coming days.

'Tell me more about the Messenger then. Why is it so special?' Barry asked changing the subject.

'Fuck me mate. You want to see it. It's unbelievable.' Barry was urging me to go on.

'As you know, on Valiant, five of us were cramped into the manoeuvring room.' Barry nodded 'We had a TG (Turbo Generating) tiff (short for Artificer) and a stoker. A MMS (Main Machinery Space) watch-keeper with his stoker and, of course, the Motor Room EM (Electrical Mechanic). That's 10 people. Minimum.' I was looking at Barry as I went on. 'Messenger has three.'

'Three where?' Barry asked.

'That's it. Three back aft.'

'Three? You're fucking joking me.'

'I'm not. A Nuclear Chief of the Watch (NCOW) in the Propulsion Control Centre (PCC) - no longer called the Manoeuvring room. He has an assistant, sort of TG Tiff qualified who looks after all the spaces and we have a Junior Rate who does whatever we say.' Barry was looking at me in disbelief. I added to his disbelief 'And I don't even have to stay in the Propulsion Control Centre! I can even wander Fwd if I want to.'

'Nah. You are pissing me about man. That's not possible. It's fucking dangerous!'

'Safe as houses. It's all automatic!' Barry was looking hard into my face and a curly lock of his hair had fallen on his eyebrow. His lips were tight and his whole bearing was one of confrontation. 'Barry remember flashing evaps (short for evaporators to convert sea water to pure water)? Remember how the NCOW would order this just before the end of the watch and the MMS watch-keeper would be pissed off as they all hated doing it?' Barry was still looking at me hard; in a challenging way. 'Now you just flick a switch and it does it all by itself.' Barry exploded.

'Fuck off Clarkie' he said as he threw his knife and fork down 'You're a fucking wind-up merchant. Always fucking have been and always fucking will be. You twat.' he added finally.

'We have three Nuclear missiles on board in tubes behind the conning tower.'

'Fuck off Clarkie I knew I'd get no sense out of you' Barry was losing patience and getting ready to leave.

'Barry, if I'm right will you pay my next month's bar bill? If I'm wrong, I'll pay yours.'

Barry fell silent. He knew I would not make such a rash bet. He knew we were both heavy drinkers and our bar bills were significant. He also knew we had lost a big chunk our pay, to court orders to our ex-wives, so to be burdened with an extra bar bill would be crippling.

'You really not bull-shitting me Clarkie?' He asked meekly but still somewhat unbelieving.

'Barry.' I said rather sarcastically 'Would I ever bull-shit you.' He was shaking his head and I could tell he still didn't know if he could trust me or not. 'I don't suppose you would believe that during our speed trials across the Atlantic we achieved a speed greater than 100 miles an hour.'

'Fuck off Clark.' then he stood up. We gathered our things and left the table. 'Fucking wind up merchant.' I decided to change the conversation.

'I'll meet you outside in 10 minutes and we'll go down the boat together. You need a special pass which we can get on the way.' Barry looked a bit sheepish. 'Cheer up.' I said slapping him on the back in a gesture of friendship.

We dodged the rain and arrived on the jetty by the Submarine. It had its own space which was fenced off from the rest. Security was tighter than that given to the Polaris submarines. I got a temporary pass for Barry. The fence was also covered with a fine nylon matting to keep this section of jetty out of sight of prying eyes. 'I have to report to a Mr John Smith on board.' Barry told me 'Is he a civvy?'

'Don't really know. Used to be a commander but he designed and built this boat. I was with him in Philli and he came over with us. He's now Head of Submarine Security. I'll introduce you to him later.'

We went down the forward access hatch which deposited us at the forward end of the control room. To go forward would bring us to the stewards' cubicle, the Captain's cabin and the wardroom. Next to this is the sound room with its array of sonar screens.

We walked through the control room and I pointed out to him the missile control section. There were three identical panels, one for each missile and one for fire control. These were locked behind removable transparent screens. Barry stopped in his tracks. He was first taken by the brightness of the compartment. All panels were of a light cream colour as opposed to the black and darkness of other submarines he had served on. Bulkheads and the deck-head were flusher and more devoid of the clutter which we had all become accustomed to. Apart from the Missile control section a large control panel was situated on the other side of the control room. This had control of all functions fwd; hydraulic pumps, air compressors, electrolysers (to make oxygen), CO2 Scrubbers (to get rid of CO2), ventilation and air-conditioning, periscopes and all other ancillary systems - bilge and trim pumps etc.

In the corner of this panel was a section controlling the rudder and hydroplanes. These could be controlled by small toggle switches and a repeat indicator, above each one, indicated the actual position. Submarine speed could also be controlled. There was also a changeover switch which I pointed to 'Look, you can select depth and bearing and switch to automatic.' Barry looked with wide eyes of incredulity 'Fucking auto pilot.' A repeat of this small panel was at the periscope section so the guy looking through the scope had direct control.

We completed our journey through the control room and was then confronted by the fwd tunnel door. This opened into the tunnel which gave access from fwd to aft and gave safe transport across the Reactor compartment. There was also a door at the aft end of the tunnel which opened to the propulsion sections of the submarine. Each door was hydraulically controlled and only one door could be opened at any one time.

An access ladder to our right led us down to the accommodation section. Walking fwd in the passage-way led us past the junior rates mess and bunk space; the senior rates mess and bunk space; a variety of small offices and then to another hydraulic door which lead in to the torpedo compartment. We stopped at the senior rates mess and went in and sat at an empty table. 'Good morning Chris.' Master Chief Elmore greeted me.

'Morning Hank.' I replied. He turned back to his conversation with two senior Petty Officers of the USN.

'Yanks, I know.' I could see the questions in Barry's eyes as I laid a hand on his arm as a sort of reassurance. 'We came over from Philli with just one watch from the UK. The rest of the crew were USN servers. I qualified mainly in a simulator and you will have to go over and do the same. Eventually we will have a full crew. After some sea trials all these guys will go, and we will have full control.' I explained.

Although the Messenger had a bar it was not permitted for the US Navy to drink alcohol on their ships. That's why they loved to get an invitation on board one of our vessels, so they could drink our beer. They always got pissed because one, they had abstained for a long time and two, the beer was really strong and potent. I was in the process of stocking our bar with spirits and beer. I would be the bar manager. I had held this position on other submarines I previously served on. I liked to do this because it gave me access to beer and spirits. I could get away with drinking a lot and not having to pay for much - perks of the job. I fished the books out from under our seat and spread them before us. My number was one preceded by my initials. Obviously, I had to establish the organisation. The next available number was 8. I told Barry this would be his bar number and he was to sign with his initials then the number 8. I leant down again and fished around in the drawer, from where I had retrieved the bar books and came up with two cans of McEwans ale. I gave one to Barry and we punctured the top and each took a slug. 'Not changed much then Clarkie.' Barry belched as he said it.

'Glad to see you aint either.' I replied fighting to keep the belch in.

The Cox'n poked his head around the curtain to our mess and held it to his chin. A big round face with glasses seemed to hang in the material of the entrance. He looked at our beer cans and his eyes widened. I reached down for another can. 'Cox'n, this is Chief Petty Officer Baldwin. He's just joined. Sort him out a bunk and do what ever else you do. When JS (John Smith) gets on-board take him up will you.' A hand reached from around the curtain and it took the can from me. 'It's okay Cox'n I got your number.' meaning I would note down he had purchased three beers that morning. The Cox'n disappeared from the curtain.

Master Chief Elmore stood up and dismissed his Petty Officers who were busy gathering up sheets of papers. 'Morning sir.' he said to Barry as he extended his hand 'I am Cyril Elmore of the United States Navy.' Barry took his hand and squeezed it firmly.

'Hello, I'm Barry.' Master Chief Elmore looked down disdainfully at our beer cans and then left the mess.

'Take no notice of that pratt. He'll be gone soon along with the rest of them.' I told Barry and didn't care that the other two were listening to me. 'Barry go with the Cox'n and afterwards I'll show you back aft.' Barry left, and I put the books away. I finished my beer, crushed the empty can and threw it in a gash can then left for the bunk space. In my locker I had a couple of bottles of Bells Whisky - I always had a stash somewhere. I took the empty hip flask from my back pocket and carefully filled it from one of the bottles. I capped it and returned it to my back pocket. I took a swig from the bottle before I screwed on the top and replaced it in my locker. Now I had completed the two most important missions of the morning - Beer and Spirits.

As I emerged from the bunk space the Cox'n was leading Barry down the passageway. 'Who the fuck's this John Smith then?' I heard Barry ask him.

Chapter 5

Mr John Smith

John Smith did not socialise with anyone. No-one knew very much about him. It was common knowledge that he once held the Rank of Commander and had qualified as a Submarine Captain with the US Navy.

What is not commonly known about Mr John Smith is that he was the adopted son of Lord Jonathan Smythe. Lord Smythe owned about half the land in Oxfordshire and trading companies in India, Kenya and Canada. All set up by his family some generations before. His father, like his fathers before him, had close ties to the Royal Family and was a frequent visitor to Balmoral, Windsor and Sandringham, to name but a few palaces and always attended Royal events as a privileged guest. Needless-to-say, Lord Jonathan Smythe was fabulously rich. He was happily married, so everyone said, but his wife was barren, yet she desperately wanted children, and someone had to follow in their fathers' footsteps, so it was decided to adopt, and John came into the family when he was only 2 months old. He was also named Jonathan Smythe and his mother doted on him and his father would look on with pride.

For a while it was a perfect world but when John was 10 years old, tragedy struck, and his mother was killed in a freak car accident. The poor boy was devastated. His mother was always showering him with love and attention whereas his father was more standoffish. With-in a year his father married again. It was a lady that John had seen often during his life and he always regarded her as an aunt. She had a son, Peter, who was four years younger than John and when they visited, they would play together and have great fun. Now they could spend more time together and, in some way, this compensated for the loss of his mother. His new mother was cold towards him, but John could understand that – he was not her flesh and blood. This coldness had an adverse effect on John. He too became cold and hardhearted.

John enjoyed growing up in such a wealthy family. He was able to travel the world, staying in the many homes they had in so many different countries. John was always the model son and Peter also behaved impeccably. John could have whatever he wanted but he was not a spoilt brat. He understood they were different, and he never looked down upon the, so-called, ordinary people or commoners. He preferred to just not let them know.

John progressed to Oxford University, where he majored in physics. He studied hard and played hard. He would gather a group of friends and fly off to the South of France for a weekend or to Minorca where they had a yacht and he would take them sailing. John would always take a group of friends to any major sporting event where his privilege enabled him to get the best seats and vantage points. Frequently he could be seen in the Royal box at Wembley or Wimbledon or any other great venue.

As he was finishing his studies another tragedy struck the family. His father collapsed from a severe heart attack and never recovered. He died the same morning. Both he and Peter were devastated. It was a great shock. However, Peter's mother never seemed to share the same grief.

Six months later John was to have the biggest shock of his life. He learned that Peter's mother resented him and had resented his presence in the family right from the very beginning. John was called into a meeting with the family solicitor. He sat there in front of him; there was no one else in the room. 'Jonathan,' the lawyer commenced 'I have been instructed to inform you, by Lady Smythe, that you are no longer a member of this family and you must leave this house as soon as possible and in any case before the end of the week.'

John could not formulate an answer. Such was his upbringing he maintained his composure and just looked blankly at the lawyer whilst he tried to make some sense of what he had just been informed of 'Sir,' he started 'My father....'
'He was not your father.' the lawyer interrupted 'He was Peter's father.'

John was astounded 'No, you have it wrong.'

'I do not have it wrong. Peter is the Late Lord Smythe's biological son as the result of a liaison with a lady who became his wife - Lady Smythe. Peter will become Lord Smythe and inherit the family fortune, you must leave this house, as you came into it, with nothing. I have now given you the information as instructed by Lady Smythe.'

John rose from his chair and left the room. He walked through the grand hall, zombie-like, and out of the front door. He skirted the fountain and marched towards the graveled driveway. He crunched his way along the quarter mile to the wrought iron main gates. The gate keeper came out with a look of surprise on his face. He was shocked to see the expression on John's face. 'Is everything alright sir?' he asked. John looked at him blankly. As if he didn't understand the question.

'Yes,' he answered, 'everything is fine.' and he walked through the pedestrian gate and left the life of a lord behind him.

John changed his name from Jonathon Smythe to John Smith and joined the Navy. His passion was Submarines and underwater dynamics. He was fascinated by the work the Russian were doing with Super-cavitation and the development of the Supercavitation torpedo in the 1970's. The idea of a torpedo travelling more than 200 knots seemed unbelievable, but it became a reality.

John worked with the design department of Rolls Royce and Associates where he led a team and developed the first UK supercavitation torpedo. The Russian version, although travelling at great speed, had next to no guidance and had a very limited range – only about 10miles. The basic concept, a rocket motor would propel the torpedo. Part of the rocket motor's exhaust gasses is directed to the nose of the torpedo where they are expelled through nozzles. The hot gasses cause the water to boil and a bubble of steam is created. The major part of the rocket thrust pushes the torpedo forward and the bubble will totally envelope it. In effect, the torpedo becomes a missile.

John took this concept and designed a new torpedo. The new development could jettison the rocket motor when it was expended, and the remaining vessel became a fairly traditional torpedo, powered by an electric motor, supplied from Lithium Ion batteries. The nose cone would house an on-board sonar array that could then become activated. The built-in guidance system can be programmed with all known sonar signatures. Each sea going vessel makes a noise as it travels through the water – submarines included. The whole of the noise gives a unique 'signature' when recorded by sonar. A selected target can be programmed into the guidance system, whilst still in the torpedo tube of the submarine, or it could be told to seek out any number of targets and strike the first one it finds. The batteries could give a range of about 40 miles so the Supercavitation transport phase would give an overall range of up to 60 miles.

John was held in high esteem for leading this development, but he was not satisfied. He wanted to apply some of this technology to a complete submarine to elevate its speed. However, he did not air his thoughts too much as he did not have too much support for them. He did have some radical design concepts in his head.

Mr Smith knew he needed first hand experience of submarines and submarine design. He was transferred to the United States Navy where he joined their submarine service. He qualified as a Navigation Officer and then later as a Submarine Captain and was given a submarine to command which he did very capably.

As a Royal Navy Commander John was seconded to the

Submarine design centre in Idaho almost 400 miles to the nearest ocean. Based on the shore of a large lake with a depth greater than loch ness. Submarines and hulls could be tested for speed, turbulence and noise. There he learned a lot. The design of his submarine grew in his head and he knew he could make it become reality given the chance.

In the early 1980's John came back to the design department of Rolls Royce and Associates and presented them with his ideas. People were astounded by the concepts – a submarine travelling at 100mph – just seemed unbelievable. However, John was very conservative with his proposals. He knew, in theory, greater speeds could be achieved. It is true. Greater speeds could be achieved but the submarine had to be able to operate and function as an asset to the Navy. Therefore, compromises had to be reached.

Finally, his colleagues on the design team, conceded it was a workable design. However, there was no budget for a new, radical, submarine. It was true. John knew he would have to create the demand for it, then budgets could be found – as always.

During the months that followed John lobbied his MP and Admiralty. He had meetings with the ministry of defence and had planted a seed of fear in the hearts of the military men. Russia had this technology and had built high speed Torpedoes. Iran was copying this technology and God knows who else would be copying it. He reminded them, because of what the Russians started, the UK now has its own high-speed torpedo which was far superior to theirs – as far as we knew it. John urged the decision makers to have faith in his design, as they had some years before when he delivered the torpedo. However, to convert a design drawing of a torpedo into reality is one thing. But to do the same with a design of a Nuclear Submarine is another.

John desperately wanted his design to be adopted. He wanted to see it become a reality. He had one more trick up his sleeve.

After John walked away from the house of his father he never looked back. He was determined, if that was what Peter's mother really wanted, then - let it be. Other members of the family and many friends, who gave support and deplored the actions of Peter's mother, contacted John. They all implored him to fight this in the courts and to regain his entitlement, as they were all sure that he is entitled. But John considered his intact dignity would be a greater asset. He felt wealth would be returned to him when he saw his submarine as a reality. In this endeavour he contacted some of his encouragers and outlined his work and beliefs and asked if they were able to use their influence with the decision makers, so he would be able build his submarine. He won and got the support he was asking for and left it to the higher echelons to do their string pulling.

Whilst John was desperately trying to get support, he did not realise his credibility was being upheld. Government ministers had discussed this, and a delegation was sent to the USA for talks. The UK was asking for a collaboration to build this new class of submarine. The USN knew of the design concepts. They knew also of the developments by the Russians and feared what the Russians may be able to achieve. To be able to use this new submarine's greater abilities to penetrate their defences and gather such sensitive information was a real plus point.

Unbeknown to John a UK/USA agreement was reached where the Americans would build the Submarine, at a new facility in Philadelphia harbour, and Mr John Smith would oversee the build project. The costs would be shared, and the first submarine would be British. On completion of successful sea trials another submarine would be ordered for the American Navy.

John was delighted when he heard the news. He was ecstatic! However, he was not pleased that his own Government could not trust him enough to proceed with the development in Britain. He did think it was amazing how decisions can be made and, money found so quickly, when national security is threatened. He knew that a successful build would restore the wealth he had lost – the wealth he had become accustomed to in his younger days. However, he was wrong.

John moved to Philadelphia as soon as the decision was announced and assisted the design department to convert his concept into drawings, which could be used for manufacturing. Computers were extensively used to assist in this process. John was amazed at the latest technology utilised in design. The computers were also able to test systems for correct functioning and manipulate locations, piping, cabling and control positioning for their optimum use. The reactor, and its systems, remained essentially the same although it had to be re-vamped to fit into this smaller hull of this submarine. Other designers had taken this opportunity to include their designs for automation. John welcomed this because it reduced the crew that would be necessary.

He had been in Philadelphia now for two and a half years and he had seen his submarine being born. It was now in the water and almost ready for see trials. It had been christened HMS Messenger. Mr John Smith was happy with the name and with what had been achieved. He was certain, as everyone else was, that it would function well and supercavitation speed could be achieved. A one fourth size hull had been manufactured and tested in the lake in Idaho and it is generally believed a speed more than 100knots could be achieved with the Messenger.

One cold sunny day Mr John Smith sat on a small bench in one of the many marinas in Philadelphia. He huddled his neck down around the sheepskin lining of his coat. The collar was up and caressed his ears keeping the coldness away. The moisture of his breath condensed as he exhaled it into the cold air giving the effect he was smoking. In his gloved hands he held a small booklet entitled 'Visitors Guide to Toronto'. The sun was shining reflecting light that twinkled off the bright-ware of the hundreds of leisure craft moored in the marina in front of him. He sat close to a large Yacht that reminded him of the one his father had in Minorca. He was feeling melancholy as he remembered the good times he had sailing there with his parents and then later with his friends from Oxford.

He now considered himself a poor man. He could not afford such a Yacht, as the one he was now looking at. He accepted he was 'high maintenance'. He had become accustomed to living with the privilege of being the son of a Lord. Even though that was now a long time ago – old habits die hard.

Since living in the US, he had stayed in Hotels. He did not want to live in an apartment. He did not want the responsibility of making his bed every day nor cooking his own food. He certainly did not want to wash and iron his own clothes nor clean his shoes. However, he did want newly washed and pressed clothes and would never venture out without highly polished footwear. His mother, and the help within their home, had ensured this when he was young. He needed to be served. He loved the service of a good Hotel. He loved the service of First-Class air travel. All his money would be spent on First Class air travel and top Hotels. His last trip was to Brazil. He stayed in one of the best Hotels in Rio. He could look out from the Balcony of his suite of rooms as he ate breakfast there whilst enjoying the view of the Copacabana and the Ocean. He knew that whilst he took his walk around the marinas his bed would be made, the bathroom would be cleaned, the room would be vacuumed, and all his belongings would be put away neatly. His dirty clothes would be taken away, to be dealt with, and the ones taken away the day before would be returned, cleaned, ironed, folded and wrapped in a protective paper band. These would be placed neatly in the drawers provided. Fresh bottled water would be provided, and the contents of his private bar would be audited, and any deficiencies replenished.

John liked to eat in the best restaurants. He loved the service and to be pampered by the staff. The cost of these things did not worry him – provided he had the money to pay. Alas, his military salary would not allow for such a lifestyle, so he had to save for each trip. He really did not want to do this. He wanted to take these trips whenever he wanted to. In fact, he wanted these trips to be his life. He did not want to do anything else. He also wanted the big Yacht that sat in the water in front of him and glistened so brilliantly in the sun. There were so many things John wanted, and he didn't consider them too much to ask.

John was very much a loner. He liked his own company. He could always find someone to talk to if he needed to. Cafes and bars had an abundance of people waiting to talk. John did not like cinemas, theatres or opera. He didn't much like TV although he would watch, and enjoy, natural history programs; David Attenborough was his favourite.

He didn't like women either. He never, ever, considered them seriously. He never thought them capable of any meaningful discussion; they were just pretty ornaments and sometimes not so pretty. He had never had sex and almost never had any sexual urges. Sometimes he would wake up with an erection and quite liked that feeling. However, it was always coupled with the urge to urinate. Once he started to empty his bladder the erection subsided along with the any pleasant feelings. He would party with his friends, during his Oxford days, girls and girlfriends of his friends would be around. When, on one of their more exotic trips to Cannes, Costa del Sol or Minorca, these girls would be prancing around in bikinis and sometimes topless, but they never aroused any sexual feelings within him. When they paid him any attention, he felt awkward and would ease himself out of the situation. On one occasion, a drunken young lady had cornered him, when he had drunk more than usual, she tried to kiss him. She grabbed him through his swimming trunks and he pushed her away violently. He was appalled and disgusted by her action. He had no physical attraction to men or boys and certainly not children. Pornography absolutely horrified him.

John had reached a time in his life where he began to feel dismayed. He had realised some ambitions, but he was disappointed that his designs were not accepted, on their own merit, by the British government. The Admiralty had not supported him in the early days, even though he had successfully seen the supercavitation torpedo come to fruition, and that weapon is now in production and forms part of the arsenal around the fleet. He blames the British government for him having to, somewhat, GROVEL to influential friends of his late father in order to open the eyes of the government. In total contrast, the government are delighted with the outcome. They have total confidence in the capabilities of the Messenger once it gets into service – which will be quite soon now. The Government were also very pleased with Mr John Smith for his innovation and persistence to see his dream become reality. John knew this but was not comforted by it. The government could not recompense him for his endeavours. They could not pay him a bonus. He had discussed this with his MP and also written to the Prime Minister. He had discussed it with the Flag Officer Submarines, in Faslane, who was sympathetic to his argument. Basically the 'Official' answer was that he should be satisfied with the honour of having given something of true value to his nation. His name, and achievement, would become part of history. This particular morning John had read, that a British bank worker had been paid a bonus of ten million pounds! Ten million pounds! Just for doing his job. Okay, he did his job well but Ten Million Pounds! John considered he did his job well also. In fact, more than well. John accepted his name would go down in history. The bank worker's name would not go down in history. Next week everyone will have forgotten his name, but next week he will still have his ten million pounds!

John pondered what he would do with ten million pounds. If he invested wisely, he would be able to live the life style he craved. He could fly, first class, to any city he wanted to. From one city to the next and stay in the best hotels. He could go on any cruise he wanted to. He could buy the Yacht that sat in front of him. Instead he looked down at the little booklet cradled in his lap. Toronto - only about an hour away. Not much of a first-class flight. No time to enjoy anything. Not only that it's still wintertime and the place will be full of snow. He really wanted to go somewhere more exotic. Somewhere out the Far East or maybe Hawaii again; he liked Hawaii. But, he didn't have enough money. He thought again, with resentment, of the UK banker.

He hardly noticed the small, smartly dress man who sat next to him. Normally the people in the marina would be dressed in casual or sporting attire - dress more fitting to messing about on boats. He thought it odd that now there were two people, sat together, seemingly out of place.

'Hello' the man said, 'I hope you don't mind my joining you here.' His accent indicated he was a well-educated Englishman. John looked at him and saw a golden tanned round face with bright smiling eyes. There was something Asian about his features, but Britain is such a cosmopolitan country these days.

'No, not at all.' John said smiling back at him.

'Off to Toronto then.' The man said looking down at the booklet. 'Bit cold this time of year.' Echoing John's own thoughts.

'Oh.' John said just waving the book about then added 'Maybe not. Well maybe not just yet.'

'Nice boat,' the man said nodding towards the vessel in front of them.

'Yes.'

'Similar to your father's in Minorca.' John stiffened.

'How do you know about that? Do I know you?'

'Oh, I know a lot about you John.' John was now looking at him with suspicion. 'Look, can we go and have a coffee together. I have a proposition for you. It'll be warm in the 'Bollard', it always is.' John liked the idea of having coffee in a warm place. 'My name is Samir.' the man announced extending his hand to complete the introduction. John pulled the glove from his right hand and accepted Samir's extended hand and noted how warm and soft his flesh felt. The Bollard Bar was just a little way along the jetty and they walked in silence.

'Are you some sort of secret service guy or something?' John asked when they sat down together. 'Did I do something wrong. Am I in trouble? John felt he had done nothing wrong but accepted people may want to learn where he came from and what he had been doing. However, he had nothing to hide or fear.

'No, no John. No not at all but I have made it my business to know a lot about you.'

'So, what else do you know?' John invited.

'Oh, I know all about your submarine and your torpedo for that matter. I know about your family and the injustice you suffered after your father died. Terrible, all that business. I have the greatest respect and admiration for you for just walking away. Magnificent dignity.' John was only hearing positive things from this man, but it didn't explain why he knew all these things. 'You know John, if you were employed by Rolls Royce and Associates or Vickers or indeed any other engineering organisation you would have been rewarded handsomely for your endeavours with your submarine. If you had patented your ideas, you would be set-up for life.' It's as if this man had been reading his thought from earlier. 'Trouble is, the Navy, or the Government for that matter, cannot pay a bonus. The crazy thing is they don't consider they need to.'

'Well, Samir, I do agree with you but what is the point of all this?' John was showing some irritation as he confronted the small man sitting across the table from him.

'Well,' Samir started again 'there is a way that you cold get rewarded for your submarine. Rewarded handsomely.' John was intrigued and his interest in this man had just been elevated. 'Did you enjoy your time in Rio – it is a beautiful city?' John stiffened again slightly.

'Yes, I did.'

'And the Paradise Ocean Hotel, was that to your liking?' John could not help but show his surprise 'The Executive suites are exceptionally comfortable with great views.' John was searching Samir's face for any sort of clue what he was up to. 'I bet you would have loved to stay longer but it is rather expensive.' John felt offended and somewhat embarrassed because he knew that Samir knew that he could not afford to stay longer. 'If we can make an agreement you would be able to stay there as long as you wish. There or any other Hotel of the same degree of opulence.' John could only investigate his face further as mixed emotions raced around his head. 'And you could fly between the two in your own private jet.' Samir fell silent and it was his turn to search John's facial expressions, but he received no messages.

'Well, Samir. You have my attention. What do you want of me? What do I have to do?'

'When you were in Rio, you met a man who was also staying at the same Hotel. You had a few conversations with him.'

'I guess you are referring to Pat; an Irish man. Would that be correct?'

'Yes, that's right. Pat. Irish Pat. Do you remember what you spoke about?'

'Not specifically, just general chat, comments about the beach and Hotel and other places we had been to. Nothing of any great importance.'

'Nothing of great importance, you say. Do you remember talking about staying in the Hotel longer? Living there full time even?

'Well yes but only fantasising really.'

'Pat asked you what you would do to enable you to live in such a Hotel. Do you remember that?' John nodded at the vague recollection. 'You said you would kill to be in a position where you could live in such a place.' John now felt a little uncomfortable and awkward. Samir held up his hand indicating John not to speak. 'Just a quick question. If you were offered a phenomenal amount of money to commit murder, where it would be impossible to link you with the crime and there would be no one coming after you, would you do it?' there was a pause. 'It's okay John, you don't have to answer just yet.' John noted he said *just yet*. Samir seemed to change the subject. 'What is the cost of your submarine John?' he waited for a reply.

'Well Samir, if you know so much you will know how much it costs.'

'Yes, I do. Just about one billion pounds sterling.' He announced. John did not know the cost and this figure surprised him. 'So how much did the British government give you for your Submarine John?' John said nothing. 'You see John, I have referred HMS Messenger as YOUR submarine several times now and you have not corrected me. That's because YOU consider HMS Messenger as YOUR submarine. Don't you?'

'Samir, what is the point of all this?' Samir could see John was losing patience with him. He held up his hand again as if to restrain him but really just pleaded for a little more time.

'Well, your government will end up with your submarine and they pay you nothing. Now I know we are speaking metaphorically, but if you were to sell your submarine to me how much would you accept for it?' John still did not know how to respond to this little man. It would be very easy to believe he was mad, stand up and just walk away. 'John, just to humour me a little, if we say the cost of your submarine is one billion pounds and I give you say, half a billion pounds, to buy it, then you would be a fabulously rich person and I would have a new submarine at half price.' Samir had a triumphant expression on his face.

'Samir, I think you are mad.' John got up to leave but Samir grabbed his arm a pulled him gently back to his seat.

'I am not mad. My country has sent me here to learn all about you and convince you to sell your submarine to me.'

'Which country is that then?'

'You don't need to know that. That is irrelevant to this conversation.'

'Well you won't convince me to sell you anything. You seem to be living in a fantasy world.' John pulled his arm free from his grasp 'It's a ridiculous thing to think I can sell you a submarine.' John said. 'It's not mine to sell.' He said with finality and began to pull his gloves back on. Samir laid his hand on his arm again.

'I know you can't sell it to me John.' John looked at him pleased he seemed to see sense. 'But, you could steal it for me.' John was exasperated and was shaking his head with disbelief. 'You could steal it John. Quite easily. I could tell you how to do it.' John could see Samir was serious. He really was serious. Samir really believed that John could steal a submarine. John himself, was not so convinced.

'And I suppose I have to kill someone along the way.'

'Not someone. You will have to kill the crew.'

'You are crazy.' John said thinking it would end the conversation.

'One minute,' Samir begged as John rose from the seat. Samir also stood as he reached inside his buttoned-up overcoat. He produced an envelope. He pushed this envelope close to the chest of John 'Take this. Here are the details of a Swiss numbered bank account in your name. Check it out and you will see One hundred Million pounds has been deposited into that account as an introductory payment.' John stood with his arms by his side. 'Just take it and check it. If you agree to my proposition, I will immediately deposit a further one hundred million pounds with a further three hundred million pounds when the submarine has been delivered.' John hesitated. He was interested to see the contents of the envelope and indeed, check it out. At this moment he had agreed to nothing. 'Take it and think about it. If you don't want to do business with me just give it back and there will be no further contact.'

John took hold of the envelope and looked at it. He placed it between the pages of the Visitors Guide to Toronto whilst still scrutinising Samir's face. 'Okay. I'll give it some thought.' He turned to leave.

'John!' Samir called to him, holding his finger towards him. 'Don't think you can steal my money.' There was real menace in his voice and his face took on a very hard expression.

John immediately went to the Central Bank of Philadelphia and asked if they could give him a statement of his account in a Swiss bank. 'Sure.' the pretty girl said as she took the piece of paper from him. She tapped the keyboard in front of her and looked at the computer screen. After a few seconds she asked, 'What is your name sir.' He told her. 'I need to see some ID.' John fished into his pocket and came out with is shipyard pass and handed it to her. She looked at it. 'That's Fine,' then she tapped some more, and a dot matrix printer sprang into life. She tore off the sheet, when it stopped exiting the machine, and handed it to John. John looked at it and his heart raced. His name was there, and the Balance read £100,000,000.00 'Do you wish to make a withdrawal or transfer?' the lady asked.

'No. No thank you.' John answered and turned away from her smiling face.

John sat in the lounge chair of his Hotel looking down at the piece of paper. The statement of a numbered Swiss bank account with his name as the holder. The balance was £100,000,000.00.

John wanted the money. He wanted the life style it would bring. He thought of what Samir had said. He realised with this sort of money he really could buy his own private jet. He could buy the suite of rooms. He could buy any Hotel he wanted. He decided he would meet Samir again and see what he had to say further.

He met Samir two more times and came away with another one hundred million pounds, an out-line plan of action and a new job – Head of Submarine Security. This position would facilitate him recruiting the help he would need to execute his plan. He, and his helpers, would be responsible for killing an entire crew of a nuclear submarine and he didn't care.

Chapter 6

Messenger Tour

At about 11:00 that morning I checked in with the Cox'n. A lot of people were due to join the Submarine during the next few days and I wanted to see who I might know. The Cox'n showed me a list. At the top was a guy called Brian Wilson. He would be the most senior fwd guy in the Submarine. He was a Mechanical Mechanician. This means he, like me, joined as a mechanic and then after a period at sea time gathering experience and some seniority, and if selected, went on to complete a 2-year technicians training. He was mechanical discipline and I was electrical. I had never met this man before.

As I scrolled down the list the name of Chief Petty Officer Leonard jumped out at me. I had met Lanky, as we used to call him, before. He was now a NCOW. I wandered if he was still as miserable as he always was. Mind you I was now in a similar position to his then, in as much as I am now divorced and have no money. I wondered if I came across as miserable as he did then. I noted there were two more NCOW's joining making four including me and Bonker. Most watch-keeping positions had only three.

Towards the bottom of the list another name stood out. EM (Electrical Mechanic) Raymond Thames. Jock Thames. An old friend from my days on Hermes. We were junior rates together, in fact, he still is a junior rate. I could never fathom this guy out. A complete bull-shitter yet I liked him. I remember trying to woo his wife. I didn't really fancy her, but she had big tits and I'd shag anything in those days, well, nothing much has changed. Anyway, I never got anywhere with her. I would look forward to seeing Jock again even if I knew I'd be the one to buy the beer.

I gave the Cox'n the list back as Barry entered his office. 'That Mr John fucking Smith is a bit of a weirdo aint he? Is he a fucking knobber or what?' Barry was clearly unimpressed with him.

'So, what did he say?'

'Not a lot really. Just welcomed me and told me to see you who would show me around.'

'Right.' I said. 'Let's go. We'll start aft.' I led Barry out of the office walking aft and up the ladder we had descended earlier. 'You will be pleased to know the tunnel doors are the same.' I looked through the inspection window to check the aft door was shut and then let the hydraulics flow to the 'open' side of the cylinder. The heavy door swung open with a low whirring noise.

'Fuck me!' Barry said in amazement as he saw the inside of the tunnel. 'Where's all the fucking pipes and shit.'

'I told you Barry everything is automatic on this thing. The reactor systems are pretty much the same, but things have been streamlined. Almost all valves are automatic, and they carry their own battery power supply in the rare case of complete power failure.' Barry was shaking his head in disbelief.

Once through the after-tunnel door the space seemed quite open. There was a lot of machinery – power conversion equipment, transformers and controllers, but they were fairly low-level stuff. You could see over the top and to the extremes of the compartment. An American sailor sat in an armchair next to the hydraulic door that led to the next compartment aft of this one. I led Barry over to him and he stood up to greet me 'Hi Chris' he drawled 'how ya all doin'?'

'Hello Hank. This is Barry he joined us today.'

'Hi Barry, how are you?' the US sailor said extending his had in a friendly gesture 'welcome aboard.' Barry took his hand and shook it firmly.

Barry responded 'Hello Hank, I'm fine mate. Thanks.'

'My name's not Hank, It's Carl.' Barry looked confused and felt awkward as he looked from me to Carl, 'It's okay, Chris calls everyone Hank.' He had a smile when he said this clearly not offended.

‘So, what’s happening Hank,’ I asked but really wanting a rundown on the systems.

‘Not a whole bunch of things. Reactor shut down on shore-side cool-down. Power supply on and steady. All control systems running self analysis – everything checking out A-Okay.’

‘So, what you fucking doing here then Hank. Jerking yourself off.’

‘No sir.’ Carl answered smiling ‘Just keeping an eye on things.’

‘Well done. I’m just showing Barry around okay.’

‘Yeah sure no problem. We have an exclusion area raised in the escape compartment. No-one can enter, Guy working on the Telsa gear.’

‘Ah, okay.’

We turned away and Carl sat down again. ‘What’s a fucking exclusion area?’ Barry asked.

‘Barry, there’s a lot of new stuff on this boat and the Yanks are nervous about it and some of it they don’t want us to see.’

‘So, what’s this fucking Telsa gear. What the fuck does that do?’

‘Bazzer, lets come back to that. Let’s start with the simple stuff.’ Barry nodded his head, but I could tell he was uncomfortable. ‘Don’t worry it’s all automatic and we don’t have to do fuck all.’

I pointed out the panels that controlled the reactor and electrical systems. The instrumentation was simpler. Digital read-out replaced analogue dials and one read-out would scan several parameters. Should any parameter be exceeded the readout would stick on that one and an annotation, to the side, would inform the operator what action is being taken. It may be as simple as a high bilge level, so the pump would be switched on until the level receded. If the 'Start Up' level rises, in the reactor, the rods are driven in automatically. The reverse is true also. 'Look here,' I said and led Barry over to a panel close to where Carl was sitting. 'All the water tank levels.' I led his eyes further, 'All the water chemical readings. All tests carried out automatically and routinely. And here. See. Evaps. Port and Starboard. On and Off. And.' emphasising the "AND". 'An 'Automatic' position. In other words, if the Made Water tank gets empty the fucking evaporator will start all by it's fucking self.'

Barry was shaking his head in disbelief as he looked around at the instrumentation and I could see he was assimilating it to the systems he had learnt, and got used to, in the past. I had done the same thing when I first saw it. 'So, what do we do on fucking watch then?'

'Not a lot. Drink Tea and keep awake.'

Barry was able to see more familiar things with the Turbo Generators and the switchboard room. He commented at how small the Submarine was from one side to the other, the Valiant was 32 feet-ish but this was more like 25.

We went back up to the PCC and through the after hydraulic door to the Main Engine compartment. Immediately through the door two steps lowered you to the deck level. The passage way split here and access further aft could be gained by going port or starboard. In the centre were tall cabinets housing a myriad of electronics. ‘What’s all this shite then?’ asked Barry.

‘Let’s go down here first then I’ll explain’ A hatch to the side led us down to the deck below where the main engine turbines were housed. ‘Now you’ll notice a big difference here.’ I told him carefully.

‘Everything is fucking different man. I don’t know if I’m in a submarine or a fucking spaceship.’

‘Listen. Don’t upset your self. I know it’s a lot to take in.’

‘Fucking ‘ell man. A lot to take in. Talk about an understatement.’

I held my hand up for him to be quiet and led him around the back of the main turbine. I knew he would be expecting to see the giant gear box, but it wasn’t there. There was a work bench and a couple of stools. ‘Sit down a bit.’ I invited, as I reached for my hip flask and offered it to him. He showed surprise but took it and took a long swig. I did the same and re-pocketed the flask.

‘Right listen.’ I explained that Messenger did not have a propeller as all his previous submarines had. This submarine was powered by two Jet Impulse Drives (JID). These were mounted below the accommodation deck forward of the reactor compartment. I knew he wanted to know what Jet Impulse Drive was so got there first.

'A JID is like an axial flow fan but we are not moving air we are moving water. In fact, you can look at it like we are pulling ourselves along as the water passes through the inlet and outlet tubes. Just like the Torpoint Ferry in Gus pulls itself along the chains that are fixed to the banks either side.' I held my hand up because I didn't want to be interrupted. I informed him there were two inlets right, at the very front of the submarine between the banks of torpedo tubes. These inlet tubes curve down and out and each one runs either side of the lower deck. The outlet from each JID flows through outlet tubes which flow back through the reactor compartment. Underneath the turbines and out of the stern. The tubes are kept as straight as possible to reduce turbulence and promote a laminar flow and therefore increase the speed of water through the tubes. I was getting fed up seeing only astonishment on his face. 'Needless-to-say, these inlet and outlet tubes form part of the pressure hull.'

'Okay' Barry said nodding his head 'carry on.'

'Well, this system gives very little noise, at slow speed, as cavitation is just about zero.'

'And at high speed?' Barry pointed his chin at me in a questioning manner. I thought for a moment how best to answer this question.

'The speed this Submarine is capable of, noise don't matter.' Barry face turned more serious.

'What speed is that then Clarkie. And don't fucking tell me 100mph or I'll twat you one.' His mannerism only made me smile.

Bonker had such an array of facial expression he would be absolutely useless at Poker.

I ignored his question as I showed Barry where the outputs of each turbine entered a gear box and the torque was transmitted to two shafts going fwd.

'Now, tell me about this Telsa shite.' Barry commanded 'And if this is more science fucking fiction you better give me another go at that whisky.'

We both took another slug from my flask.

I lent my elbow on the bench and searched Barry's face. He was looking at me and was sweating a little. I could not keep a straight face because I knew he would not believe what I was going to say next and I was anticipating his response. He could see my smile beginning to widen and it must have been contagious as he began to smile also. 'You're not going to believe this Bazzer.' I was able to say trying not to laugh out loud.

'Fuck off you, you cunt.' Barry said, and he could not contain his laughter. We both started guffawing like two little children. The beer and whisky certainly helped but Bonker's reaction to all this new information had me in stitches. 'Come on then. Fucking tell me.'

I composed myself with some difficulty. 'Right then.' I started. Barry tried to be serious, but laughter still played about in his eyes. 'Right then.' I said again and then felt serious enough to continue. 'This submarine is invisible to any SONAR.' Barry's expression exchanged to one of seriousness as he digested what I had just told him.

'I'll believe any fucking thing now.' He looked around and continued 'They get rid of the gearbox, get rid of the fucking propeller and drive a fucking Submarine with two fucking fans, at a 100 mile an hour and no bastard can see them.'

'Hey! Bonker! Be serious. You knew this boat was different. You also knew it was shrouded in secrecy and you had to sign the official secrets act declaring that you would not talk about the Messenger or it's capabilities to anyone.' Bonker knew I was being serious now. 'You knew that so don't be too surprised at what you will learn today.'

Barry stood up, walked around a circle and took some deep breaths. 'Okay Chris. So, tell me about Telsa.'

'Well, a lot of people have been playing around with magnetism and believed many wonderful things could be done with it. A Nuclear Submarine could never exist without it. The rotating part of the Reactor circulating motor is coupled by magnetism. The rotor housing forms part of the reactor circuit and there are no electrical connections to it. It turns because of magnetism. Look at transformers. Power from one winding is transferred to another with no electrical connections! Telsa, himself was working on a system of transmitting power over greater distances but ran out of money.' Barry was listening earnestly. 'You heard of the Philadelphia Experiment?' I asked.

'The fucking ship that was supposed to disappear? Load a shite man.'

'Well that maybe. Anyhow now they came up with a system where they use pulsed magnetism and send it out in the water, along with circulating currents, and these react with the ions in the sea water and causes a sort of sonic sponge around the boat which absorbs the sound waves of SONAR before they hit the steel hull.' Barry was looking at me with a blank face. 'And that's all I know about it. Apart from the fact it works.' Barry was still looking serious. 'Why do you think they have all those big fucking cabinets you saw? For fun?'

'No Chris. Look I'm sorry man but it's a lot to take in. Does my fucking head in.'

'Don't worry Barry. I know it's a lot. And I'll tell you something else.'

'What?'

'We aint finished yet.'

We went back to the deck above, skirted the cabinets and came to the hydraulic door of the escape compartment. There was a barrier at the door with a sign hung from it clearly declaring the escape compartment was an exclusion area, and it was not permitted to be entered. Another young US Sailor sat on the Escape compartment step further barring the way in. 'Hiya Chief.' The young sailor greeted me.

'Hello Hank. What the fuck's happening then? Why all this shit?' I indicated to the barriers.

'Telsa calibration on-going.'

'I can't come in then Hank? This is Barry and I wanted to show him around.'

'Hi Barry. No, no-one can pass. You know that Chief.'

'Yeah, I know that. Just testing.' I told him, and he resumed his sitting position. 'You see Barry, it is now called the after-Escape compartment because the main motor is now fwd.'

'Yeah I see. The escape tower the same?' Barry asked me.

'Exactly the same. Some things never change. Come on let's go fwd. There's lots to see there.'

'Bye Hank' Barry called over his shoulder.

'Bye,' answered the sailor 'my names Mike, Chris calls everyone Hank.'

We went back the way we came, and as we got to the bottom of the accommodation access ladder we turned immediately to the side and through a door that Barry had not noticed before. This is called the Drive room. I pointed out the two JIDs and between them the main electric drive motor for use in emergency. 'You can see here the two tubes coming from fwd and the ones going aft.

The one going out is on the cock a bit because this shaft is the drive shaft coming from the Main Engine room.' Barry was impressed. I don't think he realised how large in diameter the drive tubes were. The Main electric drive sat between the two shafts and I rested my hand upon it. 'This motor can drive both JIDs or either one independently. Won't make the submarine go very fast though. Just for emergency use.' Barry looked around nodding his head. It was easy to take in what was happening here. 'Now we go fwd.' and with that I lead Barry out of the Drive Room. We had to stop off in the Senior Rates mess as the bar was officially open. 'So, what do you reckon so far?' I asked Barry.

'I don't know. I know you said Messenger was something special but it's a bit mind blowing. Really Chris, I would never have believed the things I have seen this morning.' Barry caressed his beer can as he spoke.

'I have saved the best 'till last.' Barry looked at me and I knew he didn't know if I was joking or not. He had seen so many new things, but he was still suspicious that I may be winding him up. We had known each other a long time and it was good to be together with this man again. I felt we could easily rekindle the good times we had had so many years before. 'Are you ready to be amazed?'

'Come on Clarkie.' he said as he sucked the remaining liquid from his beer can. 'Let's go.'

We went through the hydraulic door to the torpedo compartment. Barry stopped in his tracks has he saw the two great inlet tubes where, he thought, torpedo tubes should be.

They were in front of us at about deck level which is well below the water line. They swept back, downwards and outwards in majestic graceful curves and disappeared below the deck we were standing on. Either side of us, on racks lay the latest torpedoes ready to be loaded. Barry didn't know much about torpedoes because he had always worked back aft in the propulsion section. However, he could see these weapons were longer than normal and had a nose cone more like a rocket than a torpedo. 'These are the latest innovation in torpedoes.' I patted the one by our side. 'What do you know about them Bazzer?' I asked.

'Not a lot. They are fast. So I am told.'

'How fast Bazzer?' Barry looked at me and wondered if I was trying to trick him.

'Don't fucking tell me a hundred miles an hour.' And he faced me ready to burst out laughing, I looked at him hard and serious because I wanted him to be serious. I had other, more spectacular, things to tell him. He sensed my seriousness and the humour dropped from his face.

'300 Knots.' Barry could not comprehend this. He could not convert this to mph but knew it was fast. Before he could answer I continued. 'This is a rocket under water. A super-cavitation torpedo. Designed by our own Mr John Smith.' Barry looked at the piece of iron-mongery cradled in its rack and then back to me. 'Believe it or not but the Russians had this technology in the 1960's. They developed the first super-cavitation torpedo in the next decade – they called it VA-111 Shkval and it could travel at 200 knots! 10 years ago! I emphasised. Since then we were playing catch-up until Mr John fucking Smith was let loose with his ideas.' Barry was shaking is head again in disbelief. I led him to the nose of the torpedo. 'As you know Barry water creates so much drag on an object passing through it. Nothing travels through water faster than it does through air.'

'A fucking fish does.' Barry was quick to point out and I had to snigger at this.

'Barry! Be serious! In fact, sound travels through water faster than air but that's another thing. So, look here.' I showed him the streamlined nose section of the torpedo. At the very tip were a series of nozzles pointing backwards. 'If we eject enough air out of these nozzles, whist the rest of this shit is going forwards, then you have to accept it would be travelling in a bubble.' I could see Barry accepted this. 'If it is in a bubble then we can drive it forward with a rocket motor and use some of the rocket thrust to make the fucking bubble.' Barry was looking at me earnestly comprehending the message. 'In fact, the bit of the rocket thrust that comes out here,' tapping the nozzles with my hand, 'is fucking hot which turns the water into steam and so makes the bubble easier to create.'

'And it works?' Barry asked.

I didn't answer but just frowned at him cocking my head to one side. Again, silently asking him to be serious. 'The Russian torpedo only had a range of about 10-15 miles and had no guidance. This is different.' Going back to the other end of the machine I pointed out a section of about a third of its length. 'This is the rocket fuel. Once it is expended the torpedo has travelled at least 20 miles.

This section will then be jettisoned, and the rest is a fairly conventional torpedo. It has electric drive and a programmable selective SONAR homing system up front.' Barry was looking up and down the length of the torpedo in complete wonderment.

'300 fucking Knots Chris? How fucking fast is that?'

'Fucking fast.' I led Barry back to the torpedo compartment bulkhead and down through the hatch to the lower level. Head-room was tight here, so we huddled together between the inlet tubes to the JIDs. 'Now listen to this Bazzer my ole mate cos this will amaze ya. Basically, the speed of this boat is dependent upon the speed of the water flowing through these pipes.' And I patted the inlet tubes as I said this. If we dragged through as much water as physics would allow the boat would not be able to keep up because of the drag created by the water against the submarine's hull. The resultant speed of the boat would not be any greater than with conventional drives.' I was pleased to see Barry was paying real attention. 'These tubes' and I patted them again 'are lined with a fine mesh of bronze tubing. If we force air through them it will create a barrier of very small bubbles between the water and the inside of the tubes, then the water will be able to flow through them faster. However,' and I held my finger up to stop him interrupting. 'it does not reduce the drag of the submarine as a whole.' Barry was nodding in comprehension and agreement. 'So, around the inlet tubes, on the outside of the pressure hull, is a series of nozzles similar to those on the torpedoes which we can blast out some air and make the submarine travel in a bubble. A tube leading up the conning tower also is able to blast out the air so ensuring the conning tower is part of that bubble.' Barry seemed deflated. He looked like a man surrendering to a superior power. He knew it was useless to try and argue against me or even challenge what I was telling him. 'Now Barry, you see all these cylinder things stacked against the pressure hull. You may have thought they were compressed air cylinders, but they are not. They are rocket motors. They contain 2 different types of gases that when combined and ignited burn like no fucker's business. In fact, they explode and that's why they are used as rocket fuel. You okay with this Barry?' I asked him as he hadn't said anything for a while.

'Yes mate. It's just a lot to hoik in on the first day. I had no fucking idea. I tell you what mate – it really is amazing. I suppose Dr Spok will appear soon.' And he laughed at his own joke.

'The rocket fuel that's used with the torpedoes is solid fuel. Once it starts to burn there is no stopping it 'till it's all gone. With gas you can control it and turn it off when you want. We have a similar bunch of these in the after-escape compartment, but we couldn't see them because of the exclusion area. Guess what them lot are used for?' I waited for his answer.

'Make bubbles in the outlet tubes?' he offered.

'Great. What else?' Barry hunched his shoulders in submission.

'Propulsion.' Again, he looked at me with amazement.

'Propulsion?' he repeated 'like a rocket in a bubble.'

'You got it.'

‘Does it work?’

‘Course it works. I told you we did speed trials when we left Philli.’

‘Nah Chris, you’re not really telling me you went 100 mph.’ he said shaking his head.

‘Well, they wouldn’t say exactly how fast, but we did break the ton.’

‘Un fucking believable! Chris, you are not fucking me about are you, cos I will twat you one.’ I think now he was beginning to believe me. ‘So, what was it like?’

‘Bit noisy, like blowing ballast. Turbine revs went up because the rocket propulsion was pushing us hard. The tube intakes are not in the bubble, so water was forced down them like nobody’s business. Reactor power went down as well. A bit scary when you think we don’t have much manoeuvrability at that speed. It’s only a requirement to get out of trouble should the Ruskies find us up North or if we have to transit in an emergency.’

‘Well,’ Barry said with finality and then jokingly added ‘I’d buy you a beer, but I forgotten my bar number.’

‘Let’s go. It’s been a long day.’

Chapter 7

Mae

After the tour we went back to the senior rates mess and had a couple of cans of beer. Barry wanted me to meet his woman, but I told him I really didn't want to go into Helensburgh as I'd spend too much money; money I didn't have; then I'd have to get a taxi back. However, he convinced me and said I could stay the night there and so he could bring me back the next morning. He also told me she had a loaded fridge of beer and a cabinet full of whisky, so it was easy for me to assent.

It was still early afternoon and Barry said he needed to get his security pass sorted out and then go to the accommodation office to get a cabin allocated to him in the shore base. We agreed to meet in the Senior Rates of HMS Neptune at about 6 or 7 that evening.

I decided to go back aft again to find out what the exclusion area was all about. Carl was no longer on watch and the arm chair was occupied by another baby-faced US sailor. 'Hello Hank.' I greeted him. 'Is this exclusion area still in place?'

'Hi Chief.' the young man looked surprised to see me. 'The guy is still here but the exclusion area has been lowered.'

'So, what's he doing now then?' I asked

'Don't know Chief. Nobody knows much about the TELSA stuff.'

'Okay, I'm going to have a word with him.'

'Okay Chief.'

I went aft and skirted around the instrumentation cabinets on the upper level of the main engine room. The plastic tape and exclusion area board had been removed from the doorway and the sentry had gone. I went further aft, ducking under the escape tower, and saw the back of a guy hunched over a box with a load of cables coming from it. 'Hiya.' I called to him.

I could see I had startled him. 'God almighty! You scared the crap out of me!' he said catching his breath. 'What do you want?' he asked annoyingly.

'I'm Chief Petty Officer Clark and I'm the senior propulsion guy. I think it my duty to know what's going on back here.' He looked at me from over his shoulder.

'Oh. Okay. It's just that you spooked me man.'

'Sorry about that.' I sidled up beside him to have a better sight of the box of tricks he was using. It was the size of a small suitcase and had a number of dials and switches on the top surface. Cables came out from the sides. Some of these cables were connected to terminals inside the cabinet which had the name TELSA on the front. 'So, what's going on then?' I asked.

'Ah, just taking some Resonance reading.'

'Oh. What's that then?'

'Simple really. You know this system works with both pulsed magnetising currents and pulsed sea circulating currents.' I nodded, 'Well at different frequencies a resonance can be set up which can weaken the effective sonic screen that's being produced. The currents have to be right to react correctly with the ions in the sea water. Boring stuff really.' I nodded again as if I fully understood what I was being informed of. 'Once we find out what these combined frequencies are, the magnetising and circulating, then we can prohibit them and so, hey presto, no resonance.'

'And we remain invisible to SONAR.'

'You got it chief. You'll be after my job next.' And he giggled as he said this. 'Hi, my names Jake.' And he turned towards me as he extended his hand. 'It's good to meet you.' There was something vaguely familiar about this man and it troubled me. I was sure I had met him before somewhere.

'So why was it necessary for the exclusion area then?' I could see I had asked an awkward question.

'Well, there are other things that are not for public display.'

'I am not public.' I informed him.

'Well, Chief, I'm only following procedures. We have all signed various confidentiality documents and this submarine is 'Top Secret'. I hope you understand we all have our jobs to do.' Jake was right. Many things were on a 'Need to Know' basis only and I had to respect this. Jake was looking at me and I could tell he thought we had met before also. 'Anyway, I've just about finished here now.' And he started to disconnect his cables. I don't know if he actually had finished or that he did not want to continue with me in attendance. He would be too polite to just tell me to piss off.

'How long are you here for then?' I asked him.

'I have a lot to do so probably just before you go on your first patrol.'

'Quite a while then.' I watched him coil up the test cables and place them neatly on top of the dials and switches. He then placed a cover over it all and locked it in position. I noted the bunch of keys he had were rather large. He had many locks under his control. 'How long have you worked for TELSA Jake?' He looked at me probably wondering why I would be asking such a question. 'Were you in the Navy before-hand.' I added trying to make it easy for him and that I was not just interrogating him.

'No. I was a GI and did one tour of 'nam and that's it.' he was looking at me intently again. 'Stopped off in Singapore on the way home. You ever get there. Singapore, I mean.' Then I remembered that's where I met him. He was trapped between the Union Jack Club and a chain link fence. The fence ran between the UJC and another building. The gap tapered, narrowing, the further from the front. He had forced his way in and got stuck.

'End of the 60's. I remember dragging a GI out of a gap between the UJC and a fence.' A big smile spread across my face as I told him this.

'God dammit! Yes! It was you. You and a mate. Chris and Budgie right?'

'That's it.' I confirmed 'You took us down Bugis street afterwards.'

'Goll-ee. You saved my life that day.' He took my hand again and shook it hard. 'I was stuck there for hours man. Kept passing out. Felt sure I was going to die.' He was shaking my hand again with both his. 'I would not have lasted the night I'm sure of it.' Tears were welling up in his eyes as his memory recalled the events. 'Oh Chris, it's so good to see you again.' He said sincerely 'Where's Budgie?' he asked looking around fully expecting to see him.

'Oh, I aint seen Budgie for years. He's not a Submariner.'

We then talked about the time we had in Bugis street and how he bought us beer all night. He told me he started with TELSA shortly after his return and worked on special systems. He told me some were of a very sensitive nature and asked me not to push him for details.

We promised to get together for a beer before he would return to the US.

I went fwd and filled the hip flask again from the bottle in my locker. I took a long pull from the bottle before I pushed it back in and locked the door.

As I was sure to be able to drink some free beer tonight, I decided I could afford a couple of pints in the inboard mess before getting changed to go ashore. The mess was filled with RA's (R.A. is the designation of the ratings who live ashore in married quarters. It stands for Rationed Ashore.). The RA's would always have a few beers in the mess before going home. Once home they would not be allowed out, their wives would never allow it. If they got home late the excuse would always be, they were working late.... I had a couple of beers then left to get changed.

Barry picked me up by the main gate and we got the beady eye from the military police and the Regulating staff who were on duty. They all wondered how anyone could afford such a car. I was cushioned in soft leather as I pulled the car door shut. The instrumentation, and there was a lot of it, had a soft green glow. The car glided away, and it was as if we were flying. It was a beautiful car and I was jealous of Barry.

We drove along the Gare Loch into Helensburgh. I took a swig from my hip flask and offered it to Barry. He did the same and give it me back. We glided along by the sea to the central traffic lights. Turning left the street rolled out before us inclining gently. I took another swig of whisky and put the flask away. Somewhere, near the top, Barry turned off and swept into open wrought iron gates. He drove into an open garage and announced, 'This is it.' I didn't want to move. The alcohol gave me a warm fuzzy feeling and coupled with the soft luxurious seating I was content. Barry got out 'Come on.' he called to me.

Barry had entered a side door from the garage and I followed. I stepped into an enormous kitchen. I'd never seen such a kitchen. It had two sinks, two ovens, one high and one low. The fridge was as big as a wardrobe. Shiny marble work surfaces contrasted to natural stone flooring. Dark oak had been used to manufacture the cabinets and doors.

Barry came in from another door 'She's coming in a minute.' He said, as he opened the fridge door and gathered two cans of beer. He placed them on the work surface as he searched for an opener.

'Hello.' I heard her voice before I saw her. She had entered the kitchen from the same door as Barry, but my attention was on Barry, so I did not see her. She was a short lady beautifully formed. Short black hair set off the pale skin of her face. Bright red lipstick highlighted her thin lips and her blue eyes shone brightly at me. My jaw must have dropped open. Barry never said she was such a looker. She wore a pale blue garment, which could only be described as a nightdress. It did not hide much. Its translucency allowed me to see her nipples topping off ample breasts and there was a dark triangle lower down. Her arms reached down and held the bottom hem of the garment and she pulled it to the sides. 'Have a good look now and then you won't have to stare all night.' She then turned around and lifted it slightly revealing the underside of her buttocks. Once again, she faced me. She glided over to me, extending her hand for me to take. 'My name is Mae' she said, 'Like Mae West.' she added. I had to force myself to speak.

'Hello. I'm Chris and very pleased to meet you. You are beautiful.'

'Thank you.' she said as she danced away to be by Barry's side. He had opened the beer and offered me one hunching his shoulders in a smug fashion. He knew I was impressed with his woman.

'Take Chris through Barry and I'll rustle us up some pizza.'

I followed Barry through the same door from which he came. There was a wide passageway stretching out to our left with an imposing doorway at the end. This was obviously the front door. Either side was stained glass windows depicting flowers and rabbits frolicking around amongst them. The design, in the glass of the door, was a coat of arms but I didn't recognise it. Probably their family crest. We crossed the passageway into the lounge. To the front the clear windows gave a panoramic view of Helensburgh and the Gare Loch. Beyond, the land rose into mountains. Beyond these, I knew would be Loch Long and the Holy Loch. It was a fabulous, breathtaking, view. Two enormous sofas dominated the room. They faced each other with a long, low coffee table between them. In line with this furniture was a grand stone fireplace. The high mantle was almost the size of a railway sleeper – one giant lump of oak. The fire was ready to go but not lit. A pile of logs was stacked to the side, ready to fuel it when it would be needed.

Barry indicated me to take the sofa facing the door and he slumped down in the one opposite. I lowered myself into the soft Italian leather and mentally compared it to the comfort of the car.

‘Fucking ‘ell Bazzer. You’re a lucky fucker.’

‘Well, somebody has to do it.’ He was being smug again.

‘You know you have to go to Philli for training Baz. Great run ashore.’

‘Yeah, looking forward to it.’

‘Stacks of fanny there and they love the British matelot. Did you know that?’

‘Why’s that then?’ he asked with interest.

‘It’s a fact. When ever I’ve been to the States the women queue up for us. They literally telephone the boat and ask to meet a Brit for dinner or something.’ Barry was listening with interest. ‘All they want is a good shagging.’ I added, and continued ‘You see, it seems to me, all the Yanks want is a blow job. That’s all they go on about. If you meet any of their ships in port and chat with them, they always want to know where they can go to get a really good blow job.’ Barry was thinking about this. ‘Even the ones on board Messenger are ranting on about the same thing. You ask them tomorrow.'

'Yeah, maybe you're right.'

'I am fucking right mate. That's why the women love us because we love to fuck. They know if they trap one of us, they'll be in for a good shagging.'

'I've never been Chris, so I don't know but I'll bow to your superior knowledge.' And he was bowing his head sarcastically towards me.

'That's probably why this Mae loves you so much. It's not you mate. It's your fucking cock. You see back home she's probably fed up of giving blokes blow jobs.'

'If what you say is true maybe that's why she ended up with a Brit.'

'For sure. Women tell me – now I'm only speaking generally of course.' I gestured apology with my hands to Barry 'Women don't like sucking men's cocks.' I could see Barry thinking about this as he was drinking from his can of beer. 'Well, think about its Baz. Men's cocks are not the tastiest thing in the world. Maybe okay when you get out the shower but around Midnight after a Vindaloo and eight pints of Guinness. All that sweating and dancing around in bars. No, fuck me Barry I wouldn't want to do it. Well I wouldn't want to do it any fucking way.' Barry was looking hard at me again. 'Not only that Barry, think of the view. Women have to look at something.'

'Clark you're fucking barmy you really are man.' Barry was shaking his head at me.

'Okay, let's ask Mae if she likes giving head.'

'She don't.' Barry was quick to tell me.

'See! See what I mean. I'm fucking telling ya. All women like cock and the Yanks don't get enough of it that's why we're quids in when we get there.'

Mae then entered the room carrying a full tray. She placed it on the table between us and started to unload it. She gave us a plate each along with a knife and fork. She off-loaded a large pizza along with various dressings. 'Now, you guys okay with beer or do you want some wine?' She was looking at me and it was difficult for me to maintain eye contact. I was feeling the effects of alcohol so had to be careful.

'A drop of vino collapso would be okay.' I said. She looked at Barry, not to ask him what he wanted, but for a translation.

'Wine.' he said.

'Ah,' she said, 'I'll bring some more beer as well.' She turned towards the door and walked out. I watched every movement of each cheek of her arse as they undulated with the motion of walking.

We sat and ate pizza. Barry and I got drunk and Mae excused herself saying she was going to bed. She came to me, bent down and gave me a kiss on my cheek. She also gave me a fantastic view down the front of her flimsy dress. I watched her arse again as she left the room.

Barry followed her out then returned with a decanter of whisky. We drank it and talked rubbish for a couple of hours. The last I remembered was Barry telling me he would show me to my bed for the night. I told him I had already found it and stretched out on the sofa.

At 06:00 I awoke bursting for a piss. I rolled off the sofa and staggered to the little toilet room by the kitchen bouncing off the furniture, walls and doorways as I went. I looked at myself in the mirror. Eyes not so bad this morning, I thought. I checked my teeth and with pride noted their evenness and whiteness. The same could not be said for my tongue as I inspected it. If I had had a choice, I would not have put it back in my mouth.

My next mission was to get a can of beer from the fridge. I drank half in one go and began to feel human again if, somewhat still drunk. I looked out of the lounge window, but the view was white. Fog. I knew that as we would go lower, into Helensburgh, we would emerge from the cloud and maybe see some sun.

I cleared the remains of our meal from the coffee table and carried them through to the kitchen. I cracked open a second can of beer. I decided to replenish my hip flask from one of the bottles in the cabinet. It was whisky, but I didn’t recognise the label. It didn’t matter – it was free.

As I finished washing up Barry came down and looked disheveled as if he had slept in his clothing. ‘Come on. Let’s fuck off,’ he said. ‘we’ll get breakfast in the mess.’ He got two cans from the fridge, opened them, and gave one to me. He gulped some from his can the let out a long ‘Ahhhhhhh.... That’s better.’

Chapter 8

Crewing up and Trials

During the next few days the rest of the crew joined Submarine Messenger. I was pleased to see Lanky Leonard again and greeted him warmly when we met in the inboard mess dining room for breakfast. He sat by himself hunched over a plate full of food with a steaming cup of tea next to it. He peered up at me with a look of horror on his face; as if he had seen a ghost. 'Lanky, are you okay?' I asked with genuine concern.

'Chris.' he said and then again 'Chris.'

'Yes, it's me you old fucker. How ya doing?' Lanky was clearly disturbed.

'Yeah, I'm fine. Just got a lot on my mind that's all.'

'Still getting a load of shit from the ex then?'

'Yeah, you wouldn't believe it. Everything's a fucking mess.'

'Never mind mate. You get extra dosh on Messenger. Extra dosh always helps.'

I told him some details of Messenger, but he seemed pre-occupied and not very responsive. I told him about Barry, who had gone to Philadelphia for training and when he returned, he himself would have to go with the other NCOW. Lanky seemed to be pleased with this information and I guess he would be looking forward to a good run ashore.

I was not aware that Lanky was looking at me knowing he would be part responsible for my death. Lanky felt guilty and he swore, to himself, that had he not already spent some of the money he received for his part of the plot; he would give it all back. Lanky was remembering some of the good times we had spent together, in Plymouth, some years ago. Then he was remembering his boat in the building shed of Poole harbour. He had seen it only two days ago before he travelled north. The inboard engine was installed with a stern drive. When not in use the drive could be raised out of the water, so would not be prey to barnacles and other sea-life crustaceans, and it would not cause any drag when under way with sail. With this drive there was no penetration of the hull so no stern gland leak to worry about. He had a small cabin with a large navigation table for his charts. A galley was opposite to the navigation cabin. It was well equipped for his requirements. He was not a good cook and didn't like it much. He would live out of tins or dehydrated foods whilst at sea. His sleeping quarters, in the bow had a double bed with access from either side. The lounge was beautiful. Walnut was used throughout and soft cushioning covered the entire seating area. The upper cabin was yet to be finished and would be equipped with controls for everything: Electric winches for sails, navigation and radar equipment, his main motor and of course steering with automatic pilot.

Alwyn thought his boat was wonderful and now he was weighing up the life he could have with it and the freedom it and the money would give him. However, he had to kill me and all the others on the Messenger to realise it all. Alwyn knew I was expendable. He had no option. He knew also that when he joined Messenger, he would meet all the people who would die. He would have to speak with them, work with them socialise with them and sleep next to them. The worst thing for Alwyn was that I was the first one he would meet. If he met others first, people he had not known before, then he could begin to harden up to the fact that almost everyone onboard, who he would bump into, would die.

Alwyn was not prepared for this meeting and had to leave. As I started to explore my breakfast Alwyn got up 'I got to go Chris.' He just stood up and left. I was amazed at such strange behaviour.

'Hey lanky!' I called after him. 'I'll see you at the security cabin later. You need a pass.'

'Okay.' He said waving his hand above his head as he walked away from me.

I had no idea what was going through his mind, but I had never seen anyone react like he did just now. I guess he would be back to his normal self later on.

When I arrived on board Lanky was already sitting in the mess. His head was down in a news paper and all his attention was on the pages. I sat next to him. 'So, you got here then.' Stating the obvious.

'Yeah.' he answered not looking up from the paper. 'The Cox'n signed me in.'

'Ah. Okay. So, you got a bunk and all that stuff?'

'Nah, he said we can sort it out later in the day.' I was bending down rummaging around in the drawer beneath my seat. I came up with the bar books and spread them open in front of me. Number 13 was the next number.

'Fancy number 13?' I asked him. Some people are superstitious and don't like that number.

'All the fucking same to me.' He grunted at me. I ignored his attitude and printed his name next to the number 13 on the ledger. I reached down again and came up with two cans of beer.

'Don't tell me it's too early for you Lanky.' as I offered him a can. He looked at me and knew he was being unkind to me. His face softened as he took it. 'Did you meet Mr Smith?' I asked. Lanky immediately looked up at me and a dark shadow of horror dropped across his face. Alwyn immediately thought he'd been rumbled. He wondered why I would be asking about John Smith. I was beginning to think Lanky had a serious problem. 'Everyone has to report to this fucking Mr John Smith when they arrive. Should be on your joining instructions.' I explained to him.

'Oh. No. Not yet.' Alwyn was relieved as he discovered the question was quite normal. I thought it strange he didn't ask who Mr John Smith was. Everyone else did.

'I'll introduce you later.' We drank the beer and I took Lanky on the tour of the boat. He did not show the same surprise or emotion, as Barry had, about the new things he was seeing. He did raise his eyebrows when I told him about the automatic evaporators. When I told him we achieved a speed of in excess of 100 mph he seemed to take it all in his stride. I thought he might be on drugs or something. He certainly was not the Lanky Leonard I served with some years earlier.

As more people joined, more of the American sailors departed. The senior Yanks didn't like me much. They thought I was too impolite and offensive to them. They all thought I drank too much, and I should not drink at all on a Nuclear Submarine. The younger lads had a certain admiration for me and they liked me being around. They tuned in more with my subtle sense of humour.

With this new submarine there wasn't too much to do apart from getting familiar with its layout and systems. There was hardly any maintenance to do and no defects to fix. Most of the junior rates were engaged in cleaning – just to keep them busy. I fitted out the new bar with optics for the spirit bottles and gas pumps for the draught beer. As always, I had cushions and covers made for the beer kegs that made perfect seating for the mess. As of this morning we had 13 senior rates and all of them liked beer. More people drank beer in the mornings than coffee or tea. It was looking like we would have a very sociable mess. I was concerned about how much beer I would need to take with us when we went on patrol. Normally, at sea, everyone abstained from drinking spirits, but beer was available. Lots of people generally used the time at sea to save some money and lose some weight so they would not drink beer. It was not the case with me and there would always be a group of us who would hang one on after the movie was finished and everyone had gone to bed. Beer for breakfast was a must for me. Stowing beer barrels was always a problem. There were only so many you could keep in the mess. Space could always be found in the torpedo compartment. Messenger was a smaller submarine and we carried a number of supercavitation torpedoes, which took up more space than conventional ones. Additionally, gas cylinders of rocket fuel occupied the spaces between the frames. On the lower level there was a large locked cage that contained the characteristic glass bottles, protected by straw, in a metal surround. These contained Sulphuric acid and, when I asked about them, I was told they were free issue with the new battery. I never remember having to change the acid in the main battery. I have changed submarine batteries before and all the old cells were taken out and replaced by new ones. Each cell would weigh about as much as a man and there would be more than a hundred of them in the battery compartment. They would require a significant amount of electrolyte to fill them all. Electrolyte was a dilute solution of Sulphuric Acid with distilled water. This amount of acid didn't seem necessary and it was occupying valuable space – space I could use to stow beer barrels. I told the Engineering Officer I wanted them off-loaded. There was no reason for us to carry them. He said he would see what could be done. However, I knew he thought I only wanted the space for beer. Nothing happened. Most drinkers would volunteer to keep a barrel in their bunk. I always did and slept with my feet resting on it – not the most comfortable of positions but you got used to it. Shorter guys had less of a problem.

I didn't have much to do, day to day. In the mornings I would sit at the corner table of the mess and account for the beer and spirits consumed the day before. I would drink a couple of cans whilst I did this. I would have already filled up my hip flask from my private stash in my locker having taken a swallow or two before I recapped the bottle. I would then go back aft to see what was going on. I would be expected to know what was going on. However, not much ever was. I would see Jake, from time to time, and he would be all over the submarine. He would be messing with the gas detectors installed in the deck-heads. There was an abundance of these detectors. They were the size of a hemisphere of a cricket ball, and the surface of each was peppered with a series of small holes. Gas detectors were an important element of a submarine. There were many lethal gasses that the submarine carried and, if something went wrong, could get into the atmosphere. The Electrolysers had been upgraded in efficiency as they had been downgraded with size. The same can be said with the CO2 scrubbers. It was also necessary to always monitor the atmosphere for the gasses that should be there, and that they are there in the correct ratio. Around the edge, of each detector, was the logo – TELSA. No-one paid any attention to them and I only did so when I saw Jake working on them. 'What you up to now Jake?' I asked when I saw him on the steps with his head cramped up amongst all the pipes and cabling. 'Don't get stuck up there.' Making a joke about the circumstance of how we first met.

'Calibration Chris. Always goddamn calibration.' He would reply to me.

Occasionally I would be told there was an exclusion area in force in the aft escape compartment and when I ventured aft, I would see the hydraulic door closed with the Exclusion Area Keep Out sign hanging on it. It seemed once the young American sailors had gone no sentries were posted.

Bonker came back from Philadelphia and was full of himself about his experience. He discovered that I was right, with regard to the American lady. He shagged his way through a variety of them.

The fourth NCOW was Jack Fox. He was short with a magnificent beer belly. He had jet black curly hair and had the air of a pirate. He would always talk out of the side of his mouth. He came from Cornwall and spoke with a thick West Country accent. He was also aggressive and always looking for an argument. I took him to one side and told him he had to go to Philadelphia for pre-qualification on the submarine systems. I told him Alwyn Leonard would be going with him. I asked him specifically to keep an eye on Alwyn. I told him I was concerned about his state of mind, as he seemed to have changed so much. 'Okay, I'll do that Chris.' He assented keenly to please me.

Life was bordering on the boring. After my trip back aft in the mornings I would spend the lunch time hour in the mess where the bar was officially open. By this time, we had draught beer.

Courage Sparkling Beer was a considerably strong brew. Two or three pints in an hour would be enough for most people. Often the lunch 'hour' would be extended, and more beer consumed. I discovered I needed to sleep afterwards but it wasn't always a good idea to go into the bunk space. It would not be good for me to be caught sleeping there by the Engineering Officer or any officer for that matter. Not only that it was not a good example to set to the junior members of the mess and they were all junior to me.

As most of the Junior rates were engaged in cleaning, I detailed one of the young lads to go to the shore-side store to get an extra bail of clean rags. I told him to put this in the aft escape compartment on the lower level and as far aft as possible. I told him we would need an extra load of rags for when we were on patrol. When this arrived, I cut the restraining cords and spread the rags around on the deck plates of the lower level. This made a very comfortable bed. There were two hatches to the lower level of the aft escape compartment, one was just inside the hydraulic door on the port side the other was on the other side and as aft as you could get. The aft hatch was hidden by a large storage rack. The rack of storage bins was locked behind a mesh door. Each one of the racks was also lockable. In front of the storage rack were several electrical cabinets with the word TELSA emblazoned upon them. The aft hatch to the lower level would swing upwards from fwd to aft and the caged door, to the spares rack, would open from aft to fwd. In order for me to get my head down, with out being discovered, I had to make an alarm. I guessed that no one would use the aft hatch, probably because no one knew of its existence. I removed the deck plate directly under the fwd hatch. I discovered the bilge float switch was beneath this. This was wonderful; it gave a legitimate reason for the removal of the deck plate – inspection of the float switch. I tied a piece of string to the deck plate and also to the hatch. If someone tried to lift the hatch the deck plate would be dragged along the deck causing a great din. This would wake me for sure. If someone came down the fwd hatch I would go up the after one. Therefore, most afternoons I would sneak back to the aft escape compartment and snuggle up on a bed of rags. About an hour would be fine. I never slept more than that. No one ever came and opened the fwd hatch, so my 'alarm' never sounded.

I bumped into Ray Thames in the accommodation passageway one day. 'Hiya Jock, I heard you were joining how ya going?'

'Ah Chris. Alright s'pose.' Jock had a vacant look about him which was not that unusual. He always was vacant. I knew Jock was still an able rate – he had never climbed the ladder of promotion. He was by far the oldest rating in the junior rates mess and older than about 90% of the senior rates mess also. The passageway didn't make for conversation so just told him we must get together ashore sometime soon.

Raymond Thames was relieved not to engage in a long conversation. He had learnt I was on board and he, like Alwyn, was horrified by the knowledge that he would take a responsibility in my death. He had come to terms with the fact that almost everyone he looked at, on board, was going to die and he would be part of that act. He had become somewhat numb to this fact and had disentangled his emotions from it. To him it was just something he had to do.

In the control room Brian Wilson was sitting at the Fwd Machinery Control panel when Mr Smith approached him. 'Take this to the inboard workshop and get someone to manufacture it.' He handed Tug some sheets of paper. It was the design of a piece of pipe-work along with all the authority for it to be manufactured on a Top Priority basis. 'Take it yourself and wait for it to be done. Stow it somewhere down by the Reserve Fresh Water tank.'

'Will do sir,' Tug acknowledged respectfully. Tug, being the most senior rating fwd of the Reactor compartment, would normally pass this on to someone more junior but, in this instance, he knew he had to ensure this part was manufactured and put in position. The part consisted of a length if two-inch diameter pipe-work with a screw down valve mid-way along its length. A flange, with four bolt holes was on one end and the other end was connected to something akin to an open-ended gas cylinder. The pipe's diameter increased to 12 inches and this increased size was 18 inches long. A simple item to manufacture; a cutting and welding exercise only. It would take an hour or so to complete so Tug took the opportunity to go to the inboard senior rates mess, for a beer, and see who was around for a chat. Being on the boat depressed him, knowing what he had to partake in shortly.

He climbed the stairs and entered the bar; it was almost empty. A bit early for the RA's Tug thought. However, there was the lonely figure of Dennis Warr at the bar. Tug had passed Dennis several times on board but neither of them spoke. 'Hi Dennis. How's things pal?' he greeted him breaking an awkward silence between them.

'Hello Brian.' After a pause he went on 'What do you think then?'

Tug knew Dennis was not referring to the Messenger as a submarine but more as to what they would be part of doing.

'Getting a bit scary. How do you feel about it now?' Tug was looking directly at him searching his face for signs of emotions; guilt, fear, embarrassment or even joy. He saw nothing.

'Has to be done.' Dennis replied with resignation. Tug detected that Dennis had accepted the task he had agreed to carry out. However, he suspected that had he not spent a considerable amount of the money he would return it and be free from this burden.

'Yes,' Tug replied with the same resignation 'has to be done.'

As the weeks passed, the crew learned every nook and cranny of the submarine. Everyone had qualified in their own watch-keeping positions and we had taken the submarine to sea to finalise this training. We did more speed and transit trials. Maximum speed was recorded just using the JIDs, and the SONAR signature was recorded. At slower speeds - silent running speeds, the TELSA gear was tested, and, by all accounts, we disappeared. It was discovered the maximum JID speed could be increase slightly using some rocket fuel to create the small bubbles in the mesh of the inlet and outlet tubes. We even tried with rocket fuel creating the bubble around the submarine but the JIDs were just not powerful enough to make this an effective method of transit. However, when the full system was used with rocket motor propulsion we literally went like a rocket. A series of tests were carried out with differing amounts of rocket fuel used for the JID tubes and for the nozzles around the inlets and up the fin. Finally, the best combination was determined, and the final speed of the submarine was kept a close secret. I could never find out what that was, but we were informed it was well in excess of 100 knots (115 mph).

My relationship with SB continued during this time and I sensed Sally was getting closer to me. She wanted to see me more often, and for me to stay with her as often as I could. We fell into a routine that whenever we went out, she would pay. I apologised to her for this, but she knew the situation with my two divorces. I didn't tell her about the extra money for being on Messenger though. That financed me for the time I was not with her.

I told her about Mae and Barry and said we had been invited out together. I also told her about her husband and the wife swapping times. Sally was really interested in hearing this information. 'You like that idea then Sally?' I asked her one time when we were sitting in a lounge bar in Dumbarton.

'No. Not really. I wouldn't like to see you making love to another woman.' She was looking at me as she told me this. I knew I had to ensure there was no trace of disappointment on my face.

'That's what Mae says now. Her husband fucked off with one of the wives.' Sally gave me a knowing nod of the head.

'See, these so-called open marriages never work.' She was looking at me intently. 'Would you like to see another man fucking me then?' I knew she wanted me to be horrified and answer no. I knew that to give any sincerity to my answer it had to be immediate. So immediately I looked wide eyed at her in astonishment.

'Certainly not!' I put my arm around her and pulled her close in a show of affection. It was true, I did not want to lose our relationship. Not that I loved her, but it was very convenient for me. She was good in bed and adventurous with sex – always ready to explore and try something new. I now knew swapping was out, so I made a mental note never to propose that.

'Mae's into voyeurism now.' I told her.

'What the fuck's that?' Sally asked. She certainly was not the most intelligent of people.

'She walks around half naked at home.'

'Well, so do I. There's fuck all wrong with that.'

'Yeah but you don't walk around naked when someone comes to visit. She does. She was naked when I went round with my mate Bazzer.'

'Yeah and I bet your fucking eyes popped out.' She accused me. My eyes nearly did pop out it's true. 'She didn't go and get dressed when you arrived then?'

'No. She did a twirl and showed me everything saying I wouldn't then have to stare all night.'

'Huh. I bet you did stare all night though, knowing you.' There was a pause whilst I was thinking what the best thing would be to say next, but she continued 'What's she like then.' Now, how could I answer this. I could not tell her what I really thought. How could I tell her she was beautiful with a flat belly and tits that stick out like they should do.

'Oh, she's okay – I guess. She's short and reminds me of my first wife so it really put me off.'

'Huh,' I guessed I got away with that one.

'Barry says she sometimes goes out with just an overcoat on. Fuck-all on underneath. They go to bars and have a drink and she sits there with just the coat on.' Sally was sitting with her legs crossed. She sat up straight and reversed the position of her legs and then relaxed with her back resting again on the back of the seat. 'Have you ever done that?' I asked her. She looked sideways at me and I knew she had. 'You fucking have aint ya?' and I leant into her again with affection. 'I bet you left your knickers off today as well.' Her face went red and she lowered it to try and hide the rising blush. 'You see, you are the same.'

'What do you mean I am the same.'

'Secretly you like to flash yourself to others. You like to let them see some high thigh or even higher and pretend you don't know.'

'Shut it! Chris.'

'You do. That's why you made such a display of re-crossing your legs whilst thrusting your tits out at the same time. You know people are watching.’

‘For fuck sake Chris. Shut up.’ And she dug me in the side with her elbow.

Chapter 9

Patrol Preparations

The last of the Americans left us and the Messenger became ours. We were all proud to be part of this new submarine. We also felt very special as we were privy to information which was not generally available to the rest of the fleet. Rumours had spread that we were a 'Fast' boat, but no one knew exactly how fast. Generally, a speed of 100mph would be considered a joke. I had been asked about this whilst ashore or in the inboard mess, but I just told them it was a need-to-know basis. I know this infuriated the guys who were trying to pump me for information. Not many people know we also carry three ballistic missiles. These were loaded before we left the States.

The program now was to off-load all the used rocket motor cylinders, the ones used during sea trials, and replace them with new ones. Supplies had to be brought on board for the forthcoming patrol.

It was decided a minimum crew would go. Only three people would be required for each position and no trainees would be taken. However, we would carry 'Passengers'. We called them passengers because they were not Navy personnel. No one knew who they actually worked for, but they came on board with a load of technical equipment in aluminium boxes. They took over a small office which was shared by the Caterer, Store Accountant and Steward. Some of their equipment was located there and some more in the sound room and connected into the ships SONAR equipment. Joe Green did not like the idea of these people coming on board. The Captain thought that Joe felt his domain was being invaded and his ability being undermined. In fact, at this time of Joe's life he couldn't give a fuck about his domain nor his ability. For him it just meant more people who would die. Finally, Joe gave up any resistance and accepted what would be. At this stage he didn't know exactly how many people would die but it would be a lot. So, three of four civvies wouldn't make a difference except more dead bodies to get rid of. Joe, like the others of Mr Smith's chosen eight, were getting hardened to the task in front of them. Joe had passed through a period of doubt. In the beginning it was an easy decision. Two million pounds for him to pursue his dream of searching for Dinosaurs in Peru. He had already bought an All Terrain motor home with all the comforts of home. He had a trailer equipped with underground listening devices, underground radar and sounding devices. He had a complete library of various researchers' life-times work. He had purchased land and rights to other land there. People thought him crazy but, for him, not as crazy as giving all his money to a thieving ex wife.

I had to bundle up my bed, in the aft escape compartment, whilst rocket motors were being moved around. Deck plates had to be removed along with some escape equipment, so the cylinders could be manoeuvred in and around. After a week or so the escape compartment was restored to normal and I was able to rebuild my nest.

One day Jack Fox was on watch in the PCC and I sidled up next to him. 'So, tell me Jack, how was Philadelphia?'

'Great run ashore.' His eyes sparkled as his mind was cast back to a few weeks ago. He had grown a scraggly beard since he left, and the curly moustache curled into his mouth and, as a consequence, was permanently wet.

'So, you get your end away then?' I asked with a knowing smile.

'Fucking right. Hey man the women there are all over you. Dunno what it is mate but couldn't go wrong. Even with this fucker.' he added caressing his ample belly.

'What about Lanky. How did he get on?' Jack was reminded I had asked him to monitor what he would be doing or more importantly how he was acting.

'Dunno really. Bit of a funny guy is he.'

'How did he get on in the simulator.'

'Alright, I think. He was in the other shift so never saw he much.

The Yanks never said anything strange 'bout he.'

'Did he go shagging do you know?'

'No don't think so.' Jack paused and thought for a while. 'bit of a loner he. Told me he used to go down by the marinas as he likes boats. Don't know if he had a bit on the side on one o' them boats.'

'Maybe he's just changed, cos he never used to be like that.' I told Jack 'He was always a bit of a loner, but he always joined in in the mess. He never had any money and I think he got divorced again since then, so the situation must be worse now.' I shared this information with Jack. 'He just blanks me now and we used to be pretty good mates.'

'Dunno Chris.' Jack said again 'You should speak with that Dennis, they seem to spend a lot of time together in the inboard mess.'

'Okay mate. I will. See you later.' And then I got up to leave.

'Is every fucker on this boat divorced? Jack asked. I thought for a while and it was true. Everyone I spoke to was divorced. 'And why is everyone so fucking old? We aint got hardly no young lads.' Jack certainly gave me something to think about. It seemed the whole crew were divorced, at least once, and most were over thirty. Paul wells was a bit of a youngster but divorced.

'They all like their beer as well.' I told him as I left him on watch.

Barry and I got together often when he was not with Mae and I was not with Sally. 'Mae wants you and Sally to come out with us one time.' He had mentioned this before, but we never seemed to make it happen. 'She wants to book a table at the Golf club.' I looked sharply at Barry 'Don't worry. She'll foot the bill.' He assured me.

The Helensburgh Golf Club was a venue for the up-market people. Submariners wouldn't go there. No submariner would pay so much for beer even if they were allowed in. Submariners were not renowned for their elegant dress sense.

'Okay tell her. This weekend could be good.'

'It will have to be Sunday as I'm duty this Sat. Will Sally be okay for that?'

'Yeah. She does nothing at the weekends. I was going to stay with her on Sunday so it's no probs.'

'Okay I'll sort it with Mae.'

'I told Sally about Mae not getting dressed in the house.'

'Shit!' Barry said concerned. 'What she say?'

'Nothing much. She was surprised when I told her she didn't get dressed when I was there. I think she was a bit jealous really. I also told her that when you both go out together, she's bollocky buff under her coat.'

'Well, that's not all the fucking time for fuck sake.'

'Well I know that. Anyhow, SB told me that she has done that as well. Never done it with me in tow though.' Barry contemplated this a while.

'They're all the fucking same. Women. They come to a time in their lives when they lose all inhibitions. They're fucking teasers. Like Mae with you the other day. She must have known you'd get a hard on and have to go back on board to jerk yourself off.'

'How do you know?' I jokingly asked. 'Anyway, you are right. When I told Sally I'm sure she got turned on by it. When we went out, she wasn't wearing any drawers and made a big display of un-crossing and crossing her legs whilst sticking her tits out. It wasn't for my benefit cos I was beside her. The place was packed so some-one got an eyeful. When we got back in the car, she couldn't keep her hands off me. Never done it in the front seat of a Vauxhall Viva before.' We both had a good laugh about this.

On board I still had a problem of where I would be able to put all the beer, I wanted to take on patrol with us. I went for another look around the torpedo compartment. I was pretty pissed off the acid bottles were still there. Tug Wilson was in the lower level, so I went down to see what he was up to. It looked as though he was inspecting a water tank. 'You okay Tug?' I asked. He looked round in surprise.

'What do you fucking want?' he asked me, which I thought was a bit harsh.

'Looking for beer barrel space.'

'Well, there's none here.'

'What's this tank then?' I asked. I knew it was designated as the Reserve Fresh Water tank. 'Looks as if it's some sort of after thought. Is it empty?'

'You're not having it for beer so don't even think about it.'

'Any idea where we can stash a few barrels then?'

'Stash it in your fucking compartments. Aft.'

'Oh, okay. I don't suppose you will want to go back there to get one when you've pulled the last pint.' It was an unwritten rule that if you had the last pint from a barrel you had to get a new one and connect it the pipe-work.

'Sorry Chris. You can't stow any here.' He said with finality and had softened a little.

A few days later I awoke on my bed of rags and focused on the deck plates above me. Someone was in the Escape Compartment. I could hear some shuffling around and the rustling of papers. The sounds were only slight but seemed to be directly above me. I tried to look up through the edges of the deck plates but could see nothing. I waited for a while to see what would happen, but nothing changed. I was a bit drunk when I got my head down but I felt okay now. I sat up and my head was clear. I positioned myself below the aft hatch and lifted it slightly. What I saw did not make sense. Jake was sitting with his back to me in the space where the stores racks should be. Jake was fully engrossed with what he was doing and didn't seem to be stopping. I lifted the hatch higher and was able to poke my head through at deck level. Jake was in a small compartment. It was like a small office. There was a flickering light illuminating the interior just like the light from a television. They were not storage racks at all. They were not TELSA cabinets either. The racks and cabinet doors were disguised bulkheads for this little office. I could see Jake was wearing head phones also, so he would not be able to hear me, providing I didn't make too much noise. I raised the hatch high and carefully latched it in its open position. I then climbed up from the lower level. I stood behind Jake and he was oblivious to my presence. No matter what I did now Jake would be startled. Jake must have sensed he was not alone. He turned, and his jaw dropped when he saw me. He ripped off his head phones. 'What the goddamn!' he started. He stood and tried to turn, but space was tight. 'Chris! You know Goddamn well you cannot enter an exclusion area.'

'I didn't enter it.' I told him. 'I was already here. I sometimes take a kip down there.' And I pointed to the deck.

'Well, you shouldn't be here.'

'Well, I am,' I affirmed and was looking past him to the contents of the room. There was a TV screen there with some images dancing around on it. 'What the fuck is all this?'

'You mustn't see this Chris. You mustn't know it's here.'

'Well, I have just fucking seen it and now I know this bastard stuff is here also, tell me, what the fuck is it all about.'

'I can't tell you Chris. You can't know. Nobody knows.' Jake was upset. He was shaking his head and holding his hand out to me to prevent me approaching further.

'Jake, what are you fucking on about. Just tell me what the fuck is going on.'

'Chris. Nobody knows about this.'

'I do.' I reminded him.

'Well you shouldn't.'

'Well I do so fucking tell me what is going on.' Jake turned the chair around and sat back down in it. He held his head in his hands and I thought he might cry. 'Are you a fucking spy or something?' He was still shaking his head. 'How come nobody knows about it? Does the Captain know?' he was still shaking his head. 'Does that fucking John Smith know?'

'No Chris. Nobody knows.'

'Well Jake I know it's here and I don't know now if I have to tell the Captain or the military police.' Jake looked up at me.

'You don't have to do that Chris. Let me explain. But before I do you must know that if you tell anyone else, I am in the crap. I mean deep crap. This would cost me more than my job. I would be blamed for you being here. This exclusion area is my responsibility. I would be seen to be negligent in opening up these things without checking the complete integrity of the exclusion area.' I did not follow. I was confused why there should be such a secret room with all the electronic gear I could see inside it.

'I work for one of the most secret organisations in the United States. It's so secret that not many people know of its existence. This is a new class of submarine and I know you know that. It was built by a special agreement between your country and mine. It is designed to gather sensitive information about our perceived enemies. This submarine will probe into areas where it's very existence will be at risk.' I was listening in silence. 'All this gear here is on-board monitoring equipment. Everything that people say or do will be recorded. Everything. Do you understand that Chris?' I understood it but failed to see why. 'If anything happens to this submarine we want to know why.' Jake seemed to relax a little and resign himself to giving me satisfactory explanation. 'Look here.' He sat down and pushed the chair backwards. 'You can see this is the control room.' He allowed me to see the TV screen. I looked with interest and could see the control room. I could see the Captain chatting with Mr John Smith and there were also another couple of guys in the back ground. 'So, from here I can see what is happening in the control room.' I nodded in amazement 'With these,' and he held up the ear phones 'I can hear what's going on.'

'So, you are spying.'

'Not exactly. We are monitoring. Look.' Jake reached up to a Dial wheel – a disc of aluminium with numbered segments and a plastic knob in the centre. He clicked it round a few notches and the PCC came into view. Jake was sat in the armchair with his feet on a toolbox. He was staring blankly into space and his feet fidgeted nervously. Another few clicks, and the torpedo compartment appeared on the screen. 'There are 97 different locations that are being monitored at any one time.' I was impressed. However, I did not let my amazement show. 'All this is being recorded on these mother fuckers,' and he tapped a cabinet to his side. He flicked a switch, waited a couple of seconds and withdrew a cassette that was about three times the size of a standard VHS videotape cassette. 'This device can record all that. This device can hold up to 100 days worth of this information. When it is full it can wipe off day one then records day 101. The next day, day 2 will be deleted and day 102 recorded. These,' and he waved the cassette at me, 'are the submarines version of the aircraft's in-flight recorder. The submarine's black box. There are two identical just in-case one gets damaged or malfunctions. Each one is fire-proof, to a certain extent, pressure proof, waterproof and shock proof.'

'Well, it certainly sounds like spying to me.' I told him.

'Also,' Jake was continuing 'psychologists want to analyse the crew's behaviour during a long trip. Obviously, they need to know if there are any serious ill effects of such isolation. If the crew knew their every action was being monitored their behaviour would change.' And I knew that made sense.

'So, what fucking good is all this if the submarine goes down in

Russian waters and they get hold of it.'

'When ever any radio signal is sent from this boat, or the RADAR is used, then a very low frequency signal is sent to us,' and he patted his chest 'and all this information will be transferred to us. The information will be imbedded as a modulation of the low frequency waves. If any ordinary radio receiver picks up these low frequency waves, they will just think it interference.' I knew low frequency radio waves carry long distances, as my Dad was a Radio Ham and used to chat with people all over the world, so I understood, to some extent, what Jake was telling me.

'You can see what happens in this compartment also,' I asked.

'Of course. From five locations.'

'So, you would have seen me making my bed and everything then,'

'Well I would if I checked them, but it is not my job to check all the cameras. That's for the psychologist and the incident investigators should that it be necessary.'

'So where are all the fucking cameras then?' Jake got off his chair and gently moved me to one side. He pointed. 'There.'

'The gas detectors. I might have known.'

'They are gas detectors but also, in these round bits, are mini cameras. You can change the position of each camera, in the detector, to give the best coverage, that's what I have been doing when I say I'm Calibrating them.' Jake sat down again and looked up at me. He seemed deflated. It reminded me of the time we had pulled him free from the place he was wedged by the UJC; he had slumped down with his back leaning against the wall, his knees were drawn up and he rested his arms and head upon them. 'Chris. I'm begging you. Please keep this to yourself.' There was genuine pleading in his voice. I knew I would keep his secret but didn't tell him immediately. I wanted to know how I could take advantage of this. If I could get in here, when we were on patrol, I could eaves drop on any conversation I chose. Surely it would be a benefit to me. If nothing else, it would be an interesting way to pass the time. I could also make my bed here.

'So, somewhere on there' and I waved my hand towards the electronic gadgetry 'is me making my bed and kipping in the afternoons.'

'Yes. For sure.'

'So. I'm gonna be in the shit then.'

'No Chris, I will reset it all before I leave which will be just before you go on patrol. Unless, there's some incident beforehand.' He shrugged a stifled giggle at this.

'Look Jake. I'm going to need to know where all these fucking cameras are and where they are pointing to. I will have to walk around this boat trying not to look self consciously at them.'

'Sure Chris. I can understand that.' He seemed to relax as he gathered I would not say anything, about this equipment in this little hidden room.

'And I want to open my locker and do whatever I want in it without being filmed.'

'Absolutely Chris. Hang on.' He turned to the TV screen and clicked the plastic knob. 'This is it.' And sure-enough the corner of the bunk space came into view and my locker could be seen in the top corner of the TV image. 'Come on let's attend to it now.'

He switched off the TV screen and pulled a roller cover down over the control gear. I closed the after hatch, down to my bed, and stood on it. We both squeezed into the corner as he swung closed the dummy door to his compartment. I was amazed at the ingenuity of it. The door was a series of dummy fronts to stores racks. In front of this was a mesh caged front that completed the illusion. I noted Jake locked this into place with a padlock. He reached up and caressed the domed detector. This is the first. You see all these little holes, they are the intakes for the air to be sampled and we can place the camera in any one of them. We can put more than one in each detector if we want so we can see in two, or more, directions. Look, here is the camera in this one.' He was pointing to one of the tiny holes. Sure enough, I could see, what looked like, a small glass bead nestled inside it.

'Fuck me!' I said in utter amazement. 'That's a fucking video camera?'

'Yes Sir.' Jake affirmed. He showed me four more in the aft escape compartment. Jake told me to stand aside as he opened the hydraulic door. He didn't want anyone to see me inside the Exclusion Area. Once the door was open, he went to the PCC and told the watch-keeper that the Exclusion Area was now relaxed, and access could be gained to the aft escape compartment if need be. Jake and I went around every compartment aft and he pointed out all the cameras and indicated the direction they were pointing. We moved fwd and he repeated the exercise. When we got to the senior rates' bunk space, we stopped below the camera that was covering my locker. He reached into his pocket and fished out a special key, like a small tube, about an inch long, with small holes and slots along its length. He checked either side of the bunk space, to ensure no-one was paying us any attention, then reached up, inserted the key and then rotated the dome about 180 degrees. 'There, that should do it.'

We saved the senior rates mess until last. 'Come on, I'll get you a beer.' We sat at my favourite table and Jake indicated the two detectors in the deck head above us. One was at each end of the mess on the centre line.

'Each one has two cameras.' He told me under his breath.

We sat and drank some beer chatting about a variety of things. Jake did not know if he would be coming back after our patrol but suspected he would not. I reassured him his secret was safe with me and that I would make a special effort to behave myself in front of the cameras.

Chapter 10

A Night out

I could see Barry as I entered the inboard senior rates mess. He had a pint in his hand and was leaning on the bar with his elbows

'Hello Bonker, how ya doing.' I greeted him as I slapped him on the back, as a show of friendship.

'Hi Chris.' He said as he turned and was clearly please to see me again.

'So how was the trip? You haven't told me much about it.' Barry ordered a beer for me and paid for it.

'It was good. Clever fuckers them Yanks.'

‘What do you mean.’

‘Well that simulator. You can honestly believe you are in a boat. Our simulator here don’t move nor does the one in Dounreay. There if you fuck up it’s like being on a fairground ride. And the noise! Fucking scares you to death.’ Barry was clearly impressed.’

‘Yeah. We have a lot to learn.’ I agreed with him.

‘Chris?’ I could tell Barry was about to be serious. ‘How fast did Messenger go, in the end, on speed trials?’

‘Don’t exactly know.’ Now I was looking at him closely and he now believed all I had told him in the past and he would not be about to laugh when I tell him what I know. ‘They didn’t tell us exactly, but they said it was more than 100 Knots.’

‘Well mate. The word over there is that it went over 200 Knots!’ Now it was my turn to be amazed and disbelieving. However, I knew Barry was not joking with me.

‘Really?’ Barry nodded. ‘Fucking scary.’ I genuinely feared travelling at such a speed under water. I didn’t want to pass my fear on to Barry so added ‘Those speeds are only necessary to get the fuck out of some place ahead of their boats or ships.’ I was trying to pacify him, and also myself. ‘We just need to ramp up there for a few minutes then we can slow down, assume ultra quiet state, switch on the TELSA gear and no fucker will know where we are.’

'Yeah, I suppose.' He said in resignation, and then turned his attention back to his beer.

'So, did you get your end away?' I asked.

'Fucking 'ell man. You were right about them women. You don't have to do much. They just come to you.'

'So, tell me.'

'Well, I was walking through the dockyard, back to the accommodation, after checking out the training centre. Then this fucking great car pulled up. It was massive. Some woman wound her window down and called me over. She asked if I was a Brit. I told her I was, and she got all excited and clasped her hands on her chest. Like a little kid. She asked me if I wanted to go with them for dinner. Her ole man, I guess her husband, was driving; he was a skinny guy with a bald head. She looked a lot younger. Anyway, this woman opened the door and invited me in. She just slid along the seat and I jumped in beside her. She had beautiful legs and she didn't mind flashing them at me. It all happened a bit quick really; I didn't give it any thought. She went on about her Grandmother that came from the UK and she thought she was something special because she had some English blood. Wouldn't shut the fuck up. Anyway, the guy asked me if it was okay if we stopped on the way for a beer. Of course, I said it was okay.'

'Naturally.'

'Anyway, they pulled into a car park and we walked into this building. It didn't look like a bar but none of their bars do so I just followed. It was dark inside, and I couldn't see for a while but then my eyes adjusted. There were women dancing on the bar with no bras on! Fucking tits every where man!' Barry was gesturing with his hands in front of his chest. 'It was great! I didn't know where to look next. The woman's name was Eve and he was called Hank, would you believe it. This Eve was sitting really close up to me. She kept her hands to herself, but I thought it was a bit strange, for her to be so close. Hank kept buying beer and I kept drinking it. Finally, they said it was time to eat. We went to their house. Fucking massive place man, with gates and a long driveway. They had servants! They gave me a whisky and showed me around. They had a pool as well. Then they had a barbeque going with real fucking steaks! Next thing I know she wants to go swimming; strips off all her lagging, asks me if I want to join her and then walks into the pool. Hank just laid back in a lounger watching; not a care in the world. She asked a couple of times for me to join her, but I didn't. I tell you what mate it was fucking embarrassing.'

'Nice embarrassment mate, and then what?'

'Well, he fucked off to bed and I shagged her in the little hut they had next to the pool. She was rampant.' Barry was silent for a moment then continued. 'She said she was going to have a shower and when she left, I fucked off. I sneaked off back down the drive and got a lift back to the accommodation block by the dockyard.

'So, was that it?'

'No, she called me after a couple of days and asked if I would join them for a barbeque, by the pool, with some of their friends. Said she was sorry she left un-expectantly the other night, and thought that I would feel bad that she just abandoned me. I hadn't been out since then, so thought it might be a good idea to accept the invitation to the barbeque. Anyway, they came and collected me. Again, she sidled up in the front seat and we all sat together there. Hank stopped off at the same boozer and said he knew I liked to look at all those tits. Well, who wouldn't. After a few beers Eve, who kept herself close to me, asked if I liked making love to her. I guessed she wanted me to do it again and that's why I was invited again. She said Hank wanted me to do it again. I wasn't surprised that Hank knew what happened and I guess it was simple to think that he knew what would happen. I mean her in the pool naked and me half pissed and then he left us alone together. I guessed also that Hank had a problem and couldn't give his missus one. Anyway, she asked me if I would do it again and could Hank watch. Can you believe that!'

'Really?' I asked, with genuine amazement 'What did you say.'

'Well, before I could answer she said that Hank would give me 50 dollars if he could sit and watch.' Barry looked up at me and asked, 'What would you fucking do?' I thought for a moment. It was a bizarre idea. For 50 dollars I might be tempted. I might be tempted to bargain to see if he'd pay more. In the end I told him.

'I might be tempted but she'd have to be on top.'

'What do you mean, on top?'

'Well, just imagine it. If I'm on top pumping way with my butt in the air and Hank sat at the end of the bed jerking his rocks off, he may suddenly produce a jar of Vaseline and stab me in the fucking arse. No sir. She would have to be on top.'

'Yeah. Right enough. Anyway, I did another runner. I went to the toilet the out the fucking back door. I'd had enough of that lot. Just down a bit I found another bar. No tits in this one but I did meet another woman. She worked in a Hotel. Told me she had to make beds during the mornings and clean the pool in the afternoon. We got pissed, she gave me a lift back and we fucked around in her car for a while. I didn't shag her, but she invited me to her Hotel the next morning. She got me into one of the rooms to be cleaned and she jumped on me. When she found out I had had a vasectomy she seemed insatiable. She said her husband never gave her a good going over. She said he was too scared of having more kids. So that was it. I'd fuck her a couple of times in the morning and then lounge around the pool in the afternoon. She would supply me with miniature bottles of whisky that they normally put in the rooms. I only had to buy a couple of beers and that was it. Ended up pissed each day with an empty sac. I swapped most of my training shifts so I could do nights and have the daytimes free.'

'Nice one Baz.' I told him. 'So, she didn't give you a blow job?'

'No. You are right. She said that's all her husband wanted.'

'Told you so mate.' We paused a moment paying attention to my beer. Then Barry asked.

'How you getting on with Miss Clydebank?'

'Ah, Sally. Yeah fine. She's looking forward to meeting you and Mae. Should be a good night out.'

'Mae is looking forward to it too.'

'How you getting on with her?'

'Fine.' Then he thought a while. 'Apparently the husband's been sniffing around. She says he wants to come back.'

'Fucking hell man. That'll cramp your style. You'll have to give the Jag back.' Barry grunted at this.

'She said he got mad when she told him about me. Reckoned he'd get me sorted out.'

'Is he violent then?'

'Well, he could be she reckons.'

'Well, be fucking careful mate.'

'Yeah, well, listen have to be going. See you Sunday at the golf club.' Barry slapped me on the back as he left.

I sat staring into my beer thinking of the week ahead. It would be the last week before we went to sea on our first patrol. The plan was to remain at sea for between 90 and 100 days. Most of the crew were looking forward to it. Looking forward to a time of giving up beer for a while and saving some money. To me there seemed to be something strange with the crew. I did not feel the general camaraderie that should exist within a submarine crew. Something was wrong with Lanky Leonard. He was so stand-offish, yet he seemed to be fucking close to Dennis Warr and insist they are on watch together. The pair of them like to be together yet away from anyone else. Brian Wilson – the senior technical rate fwd - was very short and offensive to almost everyone. His big buddy seemed to be Ginge Joe Green and they looked so odd together; one like a big fat gypsy king and the other a pale faced ginger midget. Too many loners on the Messenger for my liking. However, things might change when we get to sea.

Sunday afternoon I decided to go to the boat with the premise of checking to see if everything was okay. In reality, I needed to refill my hip flask. In any case it was normal submariner tradition to spend a couple of hours on the boat before we went ashore. In this manner we could get a belly full of duty-free beer and a few tots, so we would be well fortified before we hit the town and so have to spend less when we got there. Beer and sprits on board were always very much cheaper than ashore in the bars.

Sally came to collect me later in the afternoon. I got sarcastic glances from the military police and the Regulating staff as I climbed into this aging Vauxhall Viva. I don't know if they were sneering at the comedown from me getting in the Jag with Barry or because I was with this much older woman with too much makeup. I couldn't give a shit. If it was the car then at least I was going ashore and they were stuck on duty. If it was the woman, well at least I'd be dipping my wick this evening. Either way I had reason to give them a cheery wave as we turned around and left them behind.

We stopped off at the Hotel in Rhu for a drink; it was the halfway mark to Helensburgh. Sally confessed to me she was a bit nervous about meeting Mae. She was always suspicious of rich people especially rich women. I told her not to worry about it too much. 'She's not that rich.' I tried to reassure her. Sally looked at me questioningly. 'Can't afford knickers. She never wears any.'

'How do you know.' She accused, trying to slap me playfully. 'You always looking up her skirt?'

'No.' I assured her. 'Barry tells me.'

'Huh.' She said with disgust. 'I bet you tell him I sometimes don't wear any. You fucking men are all the same.'

'You got any on today then?' I asked teasingly.

'Not saying. I might or might not.'

'Okay, I'll find out later.'

After a few drinks we continued our way to the Helensburgh Golf Club.

The car park was large and full of cars. Although it was getting late it was still light and golfers were packing their stuff away in their vehicles after having completed a tour of the course. They had clearly had a good time as there was a lot of banter, joking and laughter between them.

Closer to the club house more expensive and luxurious cars were parked. Sally steered the Viva between a Mercedes and BMW and she had a smug expression on her face. 'My car goes as good as them.' She announced. I said nothing. I wanted to get out quick, so I could run around and open the door for her. Not that I was being gallant I just wanted to see if I could peek up her dress to see if, in deed, she had any drawers on. However, I didn't get the opportunity; she was very discreet.

The doorman stopped us in the foyer and asked if we were members. I told him we were here for the restaurant and meeting friends. I did not know what name the table would be booked under so could not tell him anything else. Finally, he suggested we wait in the bar for our hosts. A little bit of a drama but he was only justifying his position on the door and exercising some authority.

I had never been in this place. It was clearly a venue for the higher income bracket. The focal point was the large windows giving a fantastic view of the golf course with the eighteenth green in the foreground and the beautifully manicured fairway leading up to it. Mature tress, and the mountains beyond, gave a fabulous backdrop to the sight in front of us. Low tables were placed around the lounge area and each had several cushioned lounge chairs with Tartan upholstery. Members were slouching, drinking wine and beer and smoking cigars. Some looked up at us with distaste. I didn't care nor did Sally. We were both pretty full of bravado provided by the alcohol he had consumed up until then.

The bar was a shiny slab of light oak. There was a shelf above with bright sparkling glasses stacked neatly upon it, just with-in reach of the bar tender whenever he should need one.

We took all this in as we strolled from the entrance across the rich pile carpet. Some small groups were standing at the bar, some leaning against it. All had drinks in hand and rubicund glistening cheeks with fixed, ridiculous smiles on their faces. Loud talking was interspersed with bursts of forced laughter. I looked for a suitable gap, at the bar, and headed towards it leading Sally by the hand. I was then stopped in my tracks. I saw a familiar form. A man leaning against the bar with his back towards us. His head seemed sunken into his shoulders as he hunched over his drink. His shirt was half tucked into his trousers waistline although they hung low on his hips like old hipsters from the 60's. The trouser bottoms were wrinkled over his shoes. Rolls of fat pudginess prevented this man ever looking smart no matter what clothes he would be wearing. As I approached, my recognition of him was confirmed although, I still found it hard to believe it. 'Jock Thames.' I said as I nudged his elbow. He looked around at me with the surprise of me interrupting his thoughts. A look of absolute horror came over his face. His wide eyes grew wider still and his slack jaw fell open. He looked at me and then at Sally. 'What the fuck are you doing here.' I asked him. 'A bit out of your price range I would have thought.' He regained control and took charge of his jaw.

'I could say the fucking same to you.'

'Yeah, well we have been invited to dinner and I'm not footing the bill.' I told him. I introduced him to Sally and explained Jock was on the same Submarine as Barry and myself and that Jock and I had known each other for about fifteen years, although we had only just been reunited on Messenger. 'So, what you doing here then Ray?' I asked again.

'Just checking the place out.' Then he turned back to his drink. Raymond Thames was horrified to see me. In actual fact he had joined the Golf Club and had played golf there, on a regular basis, for the last few weeks. Raymond Thames never thought, for one moment, that anyone from the Naval base would walk into this club and find him here. He had almost got away with it as at the weekend the Messenger would sail then, for sure, no one would find out. Ray liked me, because we had been friends for such a long time, but Ray was also burdened with the fact that he would be part of a plan to kill me. Ray had agonised over this since he joined the boat some weeks before, and since he discovered I was on board, and would be sailing with the boat, and therefore not coming back. Ray, like Lanky, Tug, Dennis, Ginge, Paul Wells, Rees Jennings and Tom Gill had to battle with their guilt knowing, as they walked around the submarine bumping into their shipmates, that these very same shipmates would all die. However, they all seemed to cope with this guilt because the other side of the coin was freedom. The freedom to pursue the activities they had only ever dreamed of before, and which were now within their reach. They had been given so much money, they trusted Mr John Smith when he said, 'Everything will be alright.' Everything seemed so plausible and simple. The eight recruits, of Mr Smith, all wanted this task to be over with. They all accepted it had to be done and they all knew they would, and could, do their bit. Raymond could not face me at this moment. 'Chris, I got a load of shit on ma mind. Please leave me alone will ya.' Ray knew he was being unkind to me and hated every minute of doing so. At this moment he found this more difficult – being unkind to me – than the idea of me being one of the many that would die.

'Okay mate. No probs.' I wanted to add that if there was anything I could help him with then all he need do was ask. However, I did not. I felt Jock would come around at some point and explain and apologise.

I led Sally away from the bar and we sat at one of the low tables in Tartan covered chairs. I knew a waiter would come and take our order. 'I guess that miserable fucker's having a bad day.' Sally said to me nodding her head back at Jock.

'Yeah,' I felt upset and hurt. I reached out and took Sally's hand for comfort. She liked that.

Later I saw Barry enter with Mae. Mae looked stunning. She wore a tight-fitting black dress that clung to her body. She had no wobbly bits, apart from her tits, nor wrinkles. Her high heels caused her to tense up her calf muscles giving that extra bit of shape to her beautiful legs. The doorman had already taken her coat from her. She saw me, and her face lit up, as she approached us, with Barry following on. We made our introductions, and all sat down again having been told we would be called when our table was ready. 'Suppose you went down the boat before you came ashore then,' Barry asked me, knowing full well I would have done so and knowing full well why.

'Standing orders.' I told him. The two girls were talking together as if they were sharing secrets. I slipped my hip flask to Barry, so he could take a good shot as I knew that's what he was hankering after.

'Barry, look there.' I indicated to the direction of the bar. 'That's Jock Thames! Would you believe it! He's never got a penny to his name and here he is slumming it in this place. Not only that, but the guy blanked me; virtually told me to fuck off.'

'Bit of a weirdo that un man. Always seems pissed. Why 'as he never been a killick (Navy Slang for Leading Hand) or anything.'

'Dunno mate. We were on the Hermes together about 15 years ago. He's always been the same. Quite intelligent though. We had some great conversations together. Got married real young; only 17 and with a kid also.'

'Always sits with that cookie boy – Jennings. Never seem to mix with the other junior rates.'

'Well, those two did the missile course together. Both went to Florida where the Polaris missiles used to be. That Bomber Wells went with them.' I could see Barry was thinking who Bomber was. 'Paul Wells the youngish PO greenie (Navy slang for Electrician), he went with them. If we have to fire the missiles those are the fuckers that do it.'

'Ah.' Said Barry 'He's another weird fucker. That Bomber Wells. Used to be a bit of an athlete. Ran for the Navy so I'm told. Now fucking drinks too much. His missus fucked off and left him also.'

'You know Barry, that fucking submarine is full of divorcees and piss heads.' We both took a moment to think about this statement and concluded it was true.

We then busied ourselves with dinner. The waiter came, took orders and left. He returned with our drinks and various plates of food. The service and the meal were excellent. We also consumed three bottles of wine and Barry and I drank two pints of Guinness each. People frowned at us when they saw the black beer being served to us at a dining table. However, we were happy in our perceived uncouthness.

Barry paid for the meal with the credit card Mae gave him and I thanked them both. Sally also enjoyed the evening and had a great time. She chatted a lot with Mae and it was funny to hear the refined American accent of Mae exchanging with the course Glaswegian tones of Sally, especially when she couldn't help but throw in the odd expletive, such was her habit. Mae invited us back for a 'nightcap'. I was pleased about this. It meant I could refill my hip flask. That-being-said I excused myself and went to the toilet, so I could finish the thing off - if I was going to steal some whisky I may as well steal a complete flask full.

From the Golf Course Clubhouse, we could have walked to Mae's house, but we all piled into the Jag and Barry guided the large vehicle across the main road, rising from Helensburgh, into a smaller road, directly opposite the Golf Club and then into the drive of Mae's house; not enough time for the engine to get warm or the air-conditioning to get cold. I sat with Barry in the front. 'Did you see that Jock Thames? He was in the private members bar. No women allowed in that bar.'

'No, I'd forgotten all about him to tell the truth.'

'The guy behind the bar told me he was a member. He also told me he paid a shit load of money to be a member as there is a long waiting list to join this club. He said he has lots of people he knows, who want to join but they have to wait – almost five years he reckons the waiting list is.' I was astounded by this information.

'Really?' I asked, truly shocked. It didn't make sense. I knew I would have to get Jock to one side, on board, and find out what the fuck was really going on with him.

As soon as we entered the house, from the garage, Mae complained about being confined in the dress. 'Un-zip me.' she commanded me. Reaching over her shoulder to the top of her dress and pulling it upwards to tighten the zip so it could be pulled downwards un-impeded. I obliged, and the flawless expanse of her back was revealed; no bra strap in sight. As she walked away, she let the garment drop, and just as it was about to testify if she wore Knickers or not, she disappeared through the kitchen door to the passageway. 'Sort the drinks out.' She called to Barry as she left.

Sally looked at me accusingly. I sort of hunched my shoulders at her as if to say, 'what did I do.'

I led Sally through to the lounge. I could see she was impressed with its size and the spectacular view through the ample windows to the front. The lights of Helensburgh twinkled below. I led her to the sofa facing the door and slumped down upon it. I raised my arm and she snuggled under it and laid he head against my chest. Barry came in with a tray with wine glasses on it and an open bottle of wine. Two cans of Mc Ewans beer seemed out of place, but they were only thirst-quenchers for him and I. Mae entered. I saw her first and, as anticipated, she wore her pale blue nightdress thingy that I had seen her wear the other time I met her. 'That's better' she said directing her comment to Sally. She spread the bottom of the garment out, as she did with me a few weeks before, as if giving a fashion show. She did not do a twirl; that would have been inappropriate. She then slumped down opposite us and told Barry 'Darling, put that gorgeous Donna Summer cassette on would you. Makes me feel so horney.' Sally seemed to snuggle up closer to me with this comment.

We had all had a great deal to drink and were all enjoying the comfort of these wonderful sofas with the sounds of Donna Summer. We were relaxed and comfortable with each others' company. I knew Sally was getting turned on – her hand was caressing my belly and her face burying deep into my chest and neck. Nothing was frantic. It was just very pleasant. However, I had to break this mood of tranquility; I needed the loo. 'Sorry Sal,' I whispered to her as I eased myself from beneath her. 'need a fucking piss.' I stood and waited whilst I found my balance before I gingerly moved forward. Mae was cuddled up close to Barry who seemed to be in another world. Mae didn't care what she was displaying to me, but I didn't let my eyes linger too long – I was aware Sally's eyes were upon me.

'Bring the whisky back with ya.' Barry blurted out as if lurching back from unconsciousness. That gave me the excuse to go to the kitchen. I took the opportunity to refill my old friend the hip flask. I placed the whisky decanter on the table in front of us along with four stubby round glasses. Mae sat up and poured us each a small measure 'To a great evening with great friends.' She toasted rather exuberantly. We returned the gesture appropriately and once again sat back in the luxurious comfort of the Italian leather. I felt I was about to fall into a deep sleep. Barry was already sleeping and snoring loudly. Mae was slouched low on the sofa facing us directly. Her legs were parted languorously and, by now, everything was shadows. I lifted my head and could see Sally had extended one leg along the sofa. She was caressing herself gently, through her skirt, on her most intimate place possible. Mae's eyes were fixed on what she was doing. It sort of seemed natural. No jerky movements and no heavy breathing. Sally was comforting herself, that's all.

Boom! Boom! Boom! There was a terrific hammering on the front door. We all jumped up. We were all suddenly awake. Barry was looking around with wide eyes like a rabbit caught in car headlights. Mae sat up pulling her clothes into a position that she thought resembled decency. Sally swung her leg to the floor, which levered her body upright and she sat to attention next to me. Boom! Boom! Boom! Again, at the front door. 'Mae, open up! I want to talk to you.' A mans voice shouted.

'God! It's Roger. My Husband!' Mae exclaimed. 'Quickly lock the garage door.' She urged Barry digging him hard in the ribs with her elbow. Barry tried to stand but could not find his balance. He sort of propelled himself around the sofa and dived for the door. I followed him to help. We went into the kitchen and locked the door to the garage. Barry leant against it and there was fear in his eyes as he looked at me 'Fuck me. The man's a fucking maniac. He wants to kill me.' I suspected Barry was being over dramatic. I went back to the hallway and Mae was at the front door.

'Roger, go away. I told you before.'

'Mae, Listen to me.'

'Roger, go away or I will call the police.'

'You are with that man. Who is that man?'

'Roger, go away. I am with friends and you are frightening them. Go away or I will call the police.'

Sally appeared from the lounge; fear and rage on her face. 'Get me the fuck out of this place.' She came to me. We were both drunk and needed each other's support to stand. We then heard loud banging on the garage door to the kitchen.

'Mae. Let me in.' Roger called again. Barry jumped away from the door as if he had been electrocuted.

Sally was trying to get her shoes on and was staggering around in the hall. 'Look.' I said to Mae. 'We're fucking going. I'll tell him it was only us. You phone the police. Don't let him in.' I held her by the shoulders, and shook her slightly, as I told her this. Tell Barry to hide. I grabbed Sally and heard more banging at the garage door. Mae opened the front door and Sally and I shot through it. I heard it slam behind us and then we were in the cool night air. We crunched our way on the gravel driveway to the front of the garage; the garage door was always open. 'Hello!' I shouted. A red faced, wide eyed, man appeared. His tie was loose and pulled to one side. His shirt was only half tucked into his trousers. He stood in front of me wobbling, with his legs spread. His arms flapped by his side. 'Party's over pal.' I told him. 'In any case only couples allowed. You'll never be let in on your own.' His speechless mouth dropped open. 'Try again next week. Every fucking Sunday's the same.' We turned and zig-zagged our way down the drive.

'That was so funny. Let's get the fuck out of here.' Sally said dragging me along.

Chapter 11

Cells

We staggered across the main road leading up from Helensburgh town centre, as we had some hours earlier, but this time by foot and in the other direction. Sally was pissed off and determined to go home. It was assumed we would stay the night with Barry and Mae, but things changed. I suggested to Sally she may have had too much to drink to be driving. 'You fucking wan' a walk back from 'ere? Cos if you think I'm too fucking pissed to drive you won't wan' a come with me. Will ya?' I certainly didn't want to walk back nor hire a taxi. I, for sure, was not going back to Mae's house. I didn't want Sally to be mad.

'No Sal. You're not too pissed. Come on let's go.' I tried to reassure her.

We sat in the car and she fired it up. The headlights shot out a yellow beam of light and she manoeuvred it around the remaining few cars, in the car park, and out onto the main road. Turning left the road swept down hill, eventually to a public toilet block at the bottom by a set of traffic lights. Off we went. The traffic lights at the bottom were red. She stopped. The streets were quiet. It was sometime early morning so not many would be expected to be about. The lights changed, and we moved off and began our left-hand turn. 'Clunk!' a noise from the transmission and we lost momentum. 'Fuck!' she said 'Not fucking now! For fuck sake!' She then thumped the steering wheel with both hands. She bumped two wheels of the car onto the kerb as it came to a stop. My heart sank also. We both knew the problem. It had happened before and twice I had to make a repair. The clutch cable had become disconnected from the clutch pedal. Not really a serious problem but a pain in the arse to re-connect. 'Fucking car.' She spat as she opened the door. 'Fucking fucking car.' and then she walked off. I had no clue where she was going. I knew there was a petrol station some short distance ahead of us but didn't know if that was her destination. Sally knew that I could sort this problem and, I guess, she knew I would.

I got out of the car and steadied myself against it. The thought of crawling under the dashboard to fix the problem did not turn me on. I clearly would have no support from Sally. I consulted my best friend. I withdrew the hip flask and sucked upon it. My eyes screwed up with the acrid taste then the warmth hit my belly. They say the second slug always tastes better, so I repeated the exercise and sure enough I was able to savour the single malt. I walked around to the driver's side and peered in through the open door. Not much room. I got on my knees and reached under the dash board following the line of the clutch pedal. I could just about feel the top and the slot where the cable should reside. I found the cable but could not marry them up. I was getting cramp. I levered myself out and stood up. There was no sign of Sally. I looked up and down the road that ran alongside the Clyde and all was quiet. I walked back to the lights and looked up the road we had coasted down. Helensburgh was like a ghost town. This time of night is always the same in Helensburgh. I dived back under the dashboard and again located the slot and cable, but the fucking cable would not go in the fucking slot. The last two times I had to do this I tried in vain to get the fucking cable in the fucking slot but had to resort to using a pair of long nosed pliers to achieve my goal. I now accosted myself to think I could do it with out the correct instrument. Again, I extracted myself from under the dash and stood allowing the blood to resume a normal circulation. The pliers would be in the boot, but it would not open. It was locked. I then hoped that Sally had not taken the keys with her. I found them in the ignition. I got the boot open and was rummaging around in the tool box when a flashing blue light illuminated the inside of the boot compartment. The whoop whoop whooping of the police siren quickly followed. The police car pulled up in front of the Viva and a policeman emerged from either side. 'What are you doing?' one of the Policemen asked, 'You can't park here.' he added before I could answer.

'I'm not parked.' I said.

'Oh.' He said sarcastically. 'Looks like you're parked to me. Car by the side of the road not moving.'

'The car is fucked and I'm trying to fix it.'

‘Really. What’s the problem then?’

‘Clutch cable. Fucking things come off.’

‘This your car sir?’

‘No.’

‘Who does it belong to?’

‘My girlfriend.’

‘What’s her name?’

‘Sally.’

The policeman looked around. ‘Is Sally here?’ I looked around as he did.

‘No.’ The policeman approached me with a serious, menacing look on his face.

‘What’s Sally’s other name?

‘Don’t Know.’

‘What’s you name?’

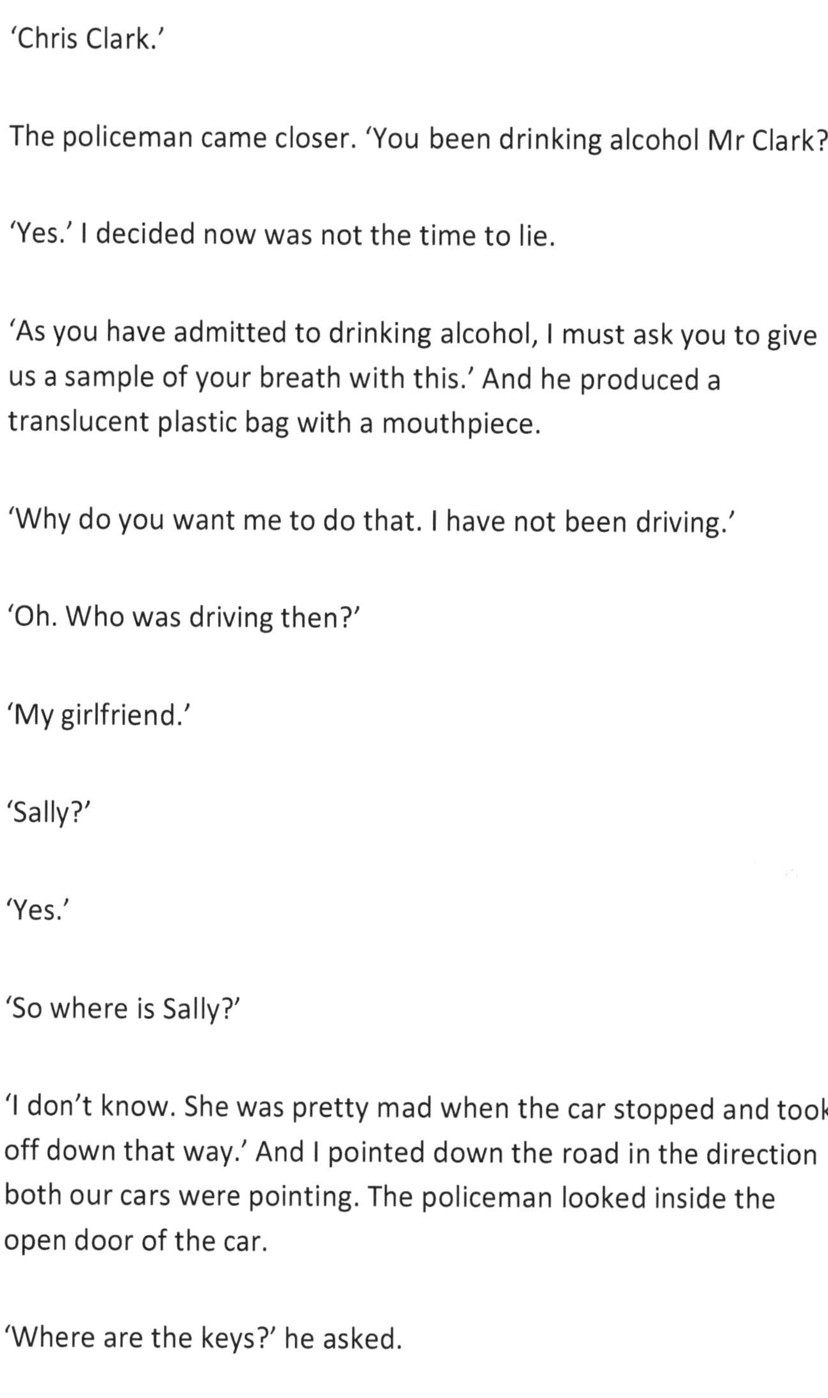

'Chris Clark.'

The policeman came closer. 'You been drinking alcohol Mr Clark?'

'Yes.' I decided now was not the time to lie.

'As you have admitted to drinking alcohol, I must ask you to give us a sample of your breath with this.' And he produced a translucent plastic bag with a mouthpiece.

'Why do you want me to do that. I have not been driving.'

'Oh. Who was driving then?'

'My girlfriend.'

'Sally?'

'Yes.'

'So where is Sally?'

'I don't know. She was pretty mad when the car stopped and took off down that way.' And I pointed down the road in the direction both our cars were pointing. The policeman looked inside the open door of the car.

'Where are the keys?' he asked.

'Here.' And I retrieved them from the boot lock.

'So, you are in-charge of this motor vehicle then?'

'I wasn't driving it if that's what you mean.' I clarified to him.

'Please,' he was offering me the breathalyser again. 'I need you to blow into this.'

'I aint doing that. I was not driving the car. It is not my car. I am not in charge of the fucking car I'm only trying to fix the fucking thing.' At this time the other policeman sidled up to his partner. Up until now he had been on the radio. He whispered a few things to him then the first one faced me again. 'Are you refusing to give a breathalyser sample Mr Clark?'

I knew now the night was going to be a long one. All I wanted to do was get my head down but that was not to be. Not for a while anyway. I didn't understand why I should be breathalysed when I had not been driving. Surely Sally would turn up but if she saw the police she would stay away. 'Look, I was not driving the car so why should I have to blow in your bag?'

'We do not know you were not driving the car, but we do know that you are in-charge of the car and you should not be drinking alcohol, to excess, if you are in-charge of a motor vehicle.' A know-it-all smugness drowned his face.

'I am not in charge of the car either.'

'You have the keys so therefore you are in-charge of the motor vehicle.'

'Fuck you.' I said to him – and it felt good. 'Fuck you and fuck your stupid bag. I aint driven no car.

Well that was it. The policeman lunged at me and threw me against the car with his forearm at my throat forcing my head backwards onto the car roof. I thought my head would come off. He tried to knee me in the groin, but I anticipated this and got my thigh in the way. He had my right arm pinned to the car with his left hand. My left hand was free, so I stuck my thumb in his eye. He squealed and then I was free. I contemplated running but knew that was a bad idea. Everything was a bad idea. The other patrol man came with a withdrawn baton which he held high and his free hand outstretched to me in the classic stop sign. 'Get in the car.' He ordered in a menacing tone whilst indicating to the police car with his head. I got in the car.

I was taken to the police station and placed in a cell. I had been in cells before and knew it to be fruitless to shout and kick and make a nuisance of myself. I was drunk enough not to worry about what would happen the following day when I got back to the clutches of the Navy. I had some misguided sense of justice that I had done nothing wrong. Poking a copper in the eye was only me defending myself. I fully expected to be visited by him later and receive a thumping.

I stretched myself out and slept. About an hour later I was awakened. A policeman, without a jacket, and there was a civilian too. The civilian said he was a doctor and he needed to take a blood sample from me. I refused to let him take one. I was adamant I had done no wrong and they had no right to breathalyse me or take my blood. I was certain Sally would eventually come forward and explain everything then I would be free to go. I really thought that, but I knew I would not be apologised to – never mind.

Some time later I awoke again. I had no watch so did not know the time. I had no shoes or tie and all my personal belongings had been taken. I wished for my cabin and the knowledge that just outside the window would be a cool McEwans. It seemed I had to go Cold Turkey with my head this morning. Later in the morning, I guessed it to be around ten, an older policeman came with a clipboard and pen. 'What time do you serve breakfast here then?' I asked. 'I don't take sugar in my tea and I prefer brown toast.' I added. The man looked at me.

'You sir are in serious trouble.'

'Why's that then?' I asked.

'You refused to give a breath sample and later refused to give a blood sample.' He told me earnestly.

'Why should I. I aint done nothing wrong.'

'Well, anyone suspected of driving whilst under the influence of alcohol is required to give a breath sample if requested.'

'But I wasn't driving. I admitted I was pissed but I wasn't driving.'

'So why refuse the breathalyser?'

'Because, in my mind it's me admitting I was driving, and I wasn't.'

'How do you come to that conclusion?'

'Well, you go out in the street this afternoon and ask any matelot, who's been in the pub, to blow in your bag and they will refuse. They have done no wrong. Just walking down the street with a few beers inside them is doing no-one any harm. They will view you with suspicion and refuse to blow in your bag. Just like I did last night. I had done no wrong and I wasn't driving the car.'

'But you were in-charge of the car. You had the key.'

'I didn't have the key. The key was in the lock of the boot lid. Your patrol man asked me where they were, and I gave them to him. I was trying to fix the car. Any of those matelots you may stop coming out of a bar with a few beers in their bellies may be in a queue for a taxi to take them home. Look in their pockets and you may well find some car keys. Does that mean they are in-charge of their cars and so subjected to a breathalyser test and subsequent conviction for drink driving. Just walking down the fucking road?'

'I have to inform you that the police are applying for a court order for you to give a blood sample. The lab can calculate back how much alcohol was in your blood last night.'

'If you take blood from me, without my consent, I will charge you with assault.' The policeman sniggered at this. 'If someone restrains me, sticks a fucking needle in me and draws blood then that's grievous bodily harm.'

'Don't make things more difficult for yourself Mr Clark.' He said in a threatening voice as he prepared to leave. 'Someone from the Navy is coming to see you soon.' He added as he was about to disappear.

'And don't forget my fucking breakfast.' I shouted after him.

Two hours of boredom passed where my headache subsided, but my belly rumbled, and I craved a can of McEwans. A policeman entered and stood in front of my cell. He had a swollen right eye. It was half closed and weeping tears. 'I wish to apologise to you for my rough handling last night.' I was completely shocked. 'It was the end of a long day.' I just stood looking at him through the bars. 'Can that be the end of that? If you make no complaint, I will also make no complaint.'

'A ha! You have done this before aint ya? If I complain you will be in deep shit.'

'I have this as evidence,' He said pointing to his eye 'and no one knows I'm here.' By now my mind was not swimming in alcohol and I was thinking more clearly. I realised I had not acted in the most diplomatic of ways. I still don't consider I have done any wrong and I certainly don't want to dig a bigger hole than I was already in.

'Okay.' And we both seemed to relax 'I need a piss and something to eat.'

'The boss wants to see you.' He pulled a key from his pocket and opened the door. He carried a pair of old bedroom slippers, which he threw down for me. I gingerly slipped my feet into them.

I was led out and up some stairs. I was allowed to use the toilets. I followed the policeman and he opened a door marked 'Interview Room' and motioned for me to enter. 'Take a seat and I'll see what I can do.'

He soon returned with a plate of sandwiches and an opened can of Coca Cola. He placed them in front of me and I dived in. The 'Boss' entered as I took my first bite. 'Do you still refuse to give a blood sample?' he asked me.

'Why should I?' I asked him.

'I am not going to play games with you Mr Clark. You are in enough trouble.'

'But I've done nothing wrong.'

'You were caught in charge of a motor vehicle, which was illegally parked, and you admitted being drunk. You refused to take a breathalyser test. You said you were not driving but no other driver was found or has come forward. The vehicle was reported stolen two weeks ago.' *Shit!* I thought. It did seem my situation was a bit grim. My mind was a whirl. Where was Sally. Sally would be able to sort all this out. Mind you, if she knew the car was stolen, she would stay away. I can't imagine Sally stealing a car! 'Furthermore, you were prosecuted for driving with excess alcohol in your blood, only seven months ago, and you are banned from driving for a further five months.' He paused whilst he let me digest the information. I was still eating the sandwich, but it seemed less important all of a sudden. I picked up the can and washed my mouth out with some of the contents. It was warm, sweet, fizzy and tasted awful. I swallowed it and immediately wanted to belch; I had to fight hard not to. 'If we add the offence of driving whilst disqualified, whilst under the influence of alcohol, to the list along with driving with no insurance then, Mr Clark, it looks likely you could go to jail.'

I was truly shocked. I was truly frightened. My situation is not good. My heart beat was raised, and I could feel it thumping against my chest. I tried to swallow again but my mouth had become incredibly dry. I found myself clenching my buttocks fearing I may shit myself. 'I was not driving the car. I was not in charge of the car. I was only trying to fix it.'

'So, who was driving the car? Where is this mysterious Sally?'

'Sally was driving but I don't know where she went.' I told him but felt my voice sounded pathetic.

There was a knock on the door and the one-eyed policeman opened it. Someone gave him a piece of paper, which he then handed to the 'Boss'. 'Your divisional officer is here.' He announced. He stood up and they both left. Lieutenant Lucas entered followed by a short fat civilian man. Lt Lucas was the Engineering Officer on Messenger. He was a newly promoted Lt and Messenger would be his first sea experience. He was a fresh-faced young man of 23 years old. He was immaculately turned out in his pristine uniform with the gold rings contrasting magnificently against the blackness of the jacket sleeves. I always wonder why they call it a blue suit. He carried his cap under his arm. I immediately stood when I saw him, but he held his hand out telling me to relax. I sat back in my chair. The short fat man carried a file of papers, which he placed on the table. They both sat down in front of me.

'Hello Chief, this is Mr Gary Osbourne.' He indicated the man by his side. 'He is a qualified Barrister and specialises in Court Martial defences.' The term Court Martial was like a stab in the heart.

'Sir. I have done fuck-all. I was not driving that car.' I blurted out.

'Hello Chief Clark,' the fat man said extending has hand to me. I took it and squeezed it. 'Well, we need to locate this 'Sally' or else the probability of culpability will fall against you.'

I told them both what had happened the previous evening with regard to us leaving the Helensburgh Golf Club car park. I told them that once the car stopped, Sally, who was pretty pissed off, marched off and has not returned. I did not know her surname or her address. I informed them I could take them to her house if need be. I also didn't know her telephone number. She was always the one who called me. I would be in the inboard mess at around six or seven o'clock, which is the arrangement we had. I also gave her the telephone number of the Messenger control room. In my defence I told them that the Dockyard Police and the duty Regulating Staff witnessed me being collected during the early evening yesterday. They would remember the car and Sally driving it.

Lt Lucas informed me that I would probably not sail with Messenger, at the end of the week, if the situation did not get better for me. If Sally did not manifest herself or decided to deny everything then I would be found guilty by the civilian courts and a Court Martial would follow. In such instances the least I could expect, from the Navy, would be to lose the rate of Chief Petty Officer. In the worst-case scenario, I could be dishonourably discharged. Mr Gary Osbourne advised me to give a blood sample then I could be transferred back to the Naval base to be kept in custody there. The two then stood and said their goodbyes. When the door closed, I have never felt so lonely in my entire life. I looked at the remaining half sandwich and the tin of disgusting liquid. I wiggled my toes in the oversized decrepit slippers. If only I could turn the clock back. But then what. I had done no wrong. The thought of a dishonourable discharge horrified me. The sheer shame of it. I would be regarded as a coward or a thief because that's how people think of it. Everything I have achieved would be counted for nothing. I could live with losing my rate. They could only bust me down to Petty Officer. There would be shame, of course, and embarrassment but I would not be the first to have to suffer such demise. I would eventually get my buttons back (Buttons on the jacket sleeve are the insignia of a CPO). Sally holds the key. She can change everything. However, that would mean her doing the right thing.

I was led back to my cell and my heart was as empty as my stomach. A medic arrived and took a sample of blood from me. 'Waste of fucking time that is.' I told the medic. 'It'll only prove I was as pissed as a fart.' The medic just looked at me, packed his things up and left.

Some time, in the early evening, I was collected from the cell and told the Navy had arrived for me. I was given my shoes, but the laces were removed. A plastic bag was handed over to the Naval Patrol man, which, I assumed, contained my personal belongings. He had to sign for these. I thought it odd that I could not check the contents. I didn't care. I was deflated. I was bundled into the back of the patrol vehicle and the door slammed behind me. I watched the sights of Helensburgh slide by through the meshed windows as we made our way back to HMS Neptune. On arrival I was transferred unceremoniously into a cell in the basement of the Administration building. A young Junior Rate gave me two blankets and a pillow. My deep depression did nothing to fend off sleep. I sank into a darkness of total isolation and slept for several hours. A tap tap tapping aroused me. The same junior rate was tapping on the cell bars with a breakfast tray. 'Want some breakfast Chief.' The young lad asked cheerfully. He didn't wait for an answer but slid the tray, on the floor, below the bars.

'Thanks.' I croaked.

Mid morning Lt Lucas came to see me. He brought with him an A to Z of Glasgow. 'Do you think you can point out where Sally's house is?' he asked me and handed me the book. As I was trying to find the right page he continued. 'Some good news for you, the Dockyard Police and the Leading Regulator both remember you being collected on Sunday afternoon. They even noted down the registration number of the car and the exact time.' I knew it was good news but not really great news. Great news would be that

Sally went to the police and explained everything. I knew that if Sally refused to say anything then the Court Martial would ensue.

‘This is it sir.’ I said pointing in the book. He handed me a pen and told me to circle it.

‘Chief, the police are investigating your case and only released you because we agreed to hold you in custody.’ My heart sank even lower. ‘However, I can arrange that you be held under house arrest. You will be confined to the inboard Senior Rates mess and your cabin. You will not be able to go anywhere else. You cannot go on board Submarine Messenger nor ashore.’ This was good news. I needed some beer and whisky, and both were in my cabin. I could also use the senior rates bar. ‘Will you agree to those conditions Chief?’

‘I will sir. Thank you.’ I was genuinely grateful.

An hour or so later a leading regulator came to collect me from the cell. ‘What’s all the fucking delay for then.’

‘What delay?’

‘My D.O. told me I’d be transferring to house arrest more than an hour ago.’

‘Paperwork. Everything has to be in order. Follow me.’ We went up one level in the administration building to the Regulating Office. The leading regulator stopped in front of a desk where a Regulating Petty Officer sat shuffling paper around. ‘Here he is.’

The Leading Reg. said and tossed more paper on the desk and then he left. The RPO did not look up. I stood waiting.

‘Can I go now?’ I asked rather forcefully.

‘Wait.’ The RPO said without even looking up. I banged my fist on the desk startling the man into some sort of response.

‘I have waited enough. Now give me my stuff RPO and I’ll be out of here.’

‘Well, well, well. You would do better to calm down.’

‘Calm down what?’ I demanded. He looked blankly at me. ‘Hey? Calm down what?’ before he could speak I continued ‘I’m the senior guy here. You will respect that. Do you fucking hear me?’ The Officer of the Watch looked at us from the far end of the office. ‘I have earned my buttons and the respect that that rate gives me, and you will respect it also.’

‘Well, you won’t have them for long, by all accounts.’ He replied rather smugly.

‘But I have them now and you will respect that and address me accordingly.’ There was a look of uncertainty on his face. ‘Do I make myself clear RPO or do I ask the Leading Regulator to write up a charge of insubordination?’ Now the Leading Regulator was looking at us in astonishment.

‘No.’ then again ‘No Chief.’

‘Okay RPO sort out what ever you need to do, give me my stuff and let me get out of here.’ I was leaning on his desk with both hands and looking directly at him as I said this. It is clear what response I needed from him.

‘Yes Chief. Right now, Chief.’ He gathered some paper and disappeared into the next office. He re-emerged with the plastic bag the police had handed over earlier. He placed a piece of paper on the desk and I could see my personal belongings listed. He emptied the contents of the bag on the desk and spread them around. He would pick up an item with one hand, run a finger down the list with the other to find the description. He then called out the description and gave me the item then crossed it off the list. A slow and deliberate process. I knew he was being perverse. When I had all my belongings, I gathered them together. I first put on my shoes then the watch. I counted the money and put it in my pocket. I picked up the hip flask and was about to put it I my pocket when the RPO reached out a hand. ‘What do you have in there then Chief?’ he asked triumphantly with a supercilious grin on his face.

‘Don’t know what it could be.’ And I handed it to him. He unscrewed the top and peered in. He then smelled it.

‘Whisky. Do you know Chief it is an offence to have in your possession a substance that is forbidden within this establishment?’

‘Well, RPO under normal circumstances it would be empty, but it was taken from me on Sunday night.’

'I'm sorry Chief but I have to charge you for being in possession of a banned substance.' He turned to the Leading Regulator. 'Give me the charge book will you Leading Reg.'

I could not believe it. I turned and saw the Officer of the Watch still observing us. 'Excuse me sir.' I hailed him over

'Yes Chief.'

'I want to charge this Regulating Petty Officer with supplying a substance which is prohibited within this establishment. I believe Sir, you witnessed this Regulating Petty Officer passing this container to me.'

'Yes Chief, I did. RPO, Chief Clark is correct. He did not bring this substance on board. It was brought with your Leading Regulator in the Patrol Vehicle. You gave it to Chief Clark so therefore Chief Clark is technically correct in saying you supplied him.' The RPO could not believe what he was hearing. He stood with his mouth open and totally lost for words.' The Officer of the Watch now turned to me. 'Chief, the RPO is correct in saying the contents of that flask are prohibited to be carried by person in this establishment. If he returns it to you, will you assure me that you will dispose of the contents at the earliest opportunity? Then nobody has to be charged.'

'Yes sir, I will.' The OOW turned to the RPO expectantly who handed over the flask.

'You would do well to apologise to Chief Clark.' he said to the RPO. The RPO's mouth opened and closed but no words came out. He was speechless. 'You would do well to apologise to Chief Clark.' The OOW said again.

'Yes. Yes Sir,' the RPO stammered and then turned to me. 'Sorry Chief,'

'No worries.' I gathered up my things, including the hip flask. 'Thank you, sir.' I said to the OOW. I had to get to my cabin to start disposing of the contents of the hip flask.

The next day, Lt Lucas came and found me in the senior rates bar, he informed me Sally could not be found. He told me the police had visited the address I had indicated, and the door was answered by a young lady who said there was no one there by the name of Sally.

Lt Lucas informed me I would not be accompanying them when the Messenger sails on Saturday. He said he was very sorry to lose me from the crew, but he had no choice in the matter. I was further informed, that Gary was fairly confident that a dishonourable discharge would be taken off the cards, at a Court Martial, because having witnesses to the fact I had been collected, in the stolen car, and there was a lady driver, whom is assumed to be the illusive Sally. It all depended upon what the Police would do. If they dropped all charges, then the Navy would do nothing; there would be no charges to answer. However, the chances of the police dropping charges were just about zero.
So, for me, the worst-case scenario was pretty much lifted. I guess I would have to hang around in Faslane, under house, arrest until

the police had decided what they were going to charge me with. I would lose my rate but then I would be sent away from Faslane so would probably end up in Plymouth. One good thing, and there always has to be a good thing, the reduced pay would mean I could not pay the ex's as much. I could get a court order to get the payments reduced.

Chapter 12

Reprise

Wednesday evening, whilst I was sat by myself trying to concentrate on the news papers' crossword, Lanky Leonard plonked himself in front of me and pushed a full pint of beer over to me. His face was beaming. 'Hi Chris.' He greeted me. 'Good to see you again. Got out of jail then.' He was smiling broadly and there was a genuine twinkle in his eye. 'Being left inboard for the trip; that's a fucking bonus.'

'Yeah. I was looking forward to saving some money though. Never mind.' I could not understand why Lanky was so cheerful all of a sudden. Since he joined Messenger, he's been really grumpy and, it seems, he goes out of his way to avoid me. 'So, why are you so fucking cheerful. You do realise I'm going to lose my fucking rate.' Lanky looked at me and a confused expression came over his face. Lanky was pleased I was not going on the trip. He was relieved he didn't have to be responsible for killing me. He had a lot of heartache having to accept I would be a victim.

‘Yeah. You are right Chris. Sorry about that.’ His expression was a little more solemn for a short while. 'Well Plymouth is a better place than this and there's always a space at the bar in the Two Trees.’

‘Yeah that’s fucking great Lanky.’ I told him sarcastically. ‘I’ll have no fucking money! Lose me buttons and the bonus for Messenger.’

‘Yeah. Sorry mate. Look, drink up and I’ll get you another.’

Things changed on Thursday morning. I had no reason to get up other than breakfast. I had finished the two cans of beer I had on my window shelf and my hip flask was empty. The inboard bar was not open for another couple of hours. I was hoping I could get down the boat on the premise that I needed to clear out my locker. I could then fill my flask and I would try and smuggle a couple of bottles of Bells inboard. It would be a risk, but I didn’t care much. I was still in a deep depression. My mind drifted to Sally. I could certainly use her now as I fondled my swelling bits. That women has the key to everything. She could tell the Police I was not driving. However, if she stayed hidden then she wouldn’t have to answer the question as where the car came from and did she steal it; did she even know it was stolen? She told me it belonged to her daughter. I heard the door of the corridor open as someone came through it. I heard foot steps approach and they stopped outside my door. Who ever it was tapped lightly on the door ‘Chief Clark?’

‘Yes.'

‘Lt Lucas wants to see you. He said he will wait by the admin building.’

‘Okay. Thanks.' I got up quickly and got dressed. Maybe it was good news about Sally. For me things could not get worse, so I had no dread in my mind. I could also get his permission to go on board and sort my locker out.

‘Morning Chief.' Lt Lucas greeted me returning my salute. ‘There has been a development. We have to go to FOSM’s (Flag Office Submarines) Office. Come on.' Something serious must have occurred for me to be summoned to go there and to be summoned by my D.O. ‘Your mate, Chief Baldwin, has broken both his legs.' he informed me. I was genuinely shocked.

‘How?’ I asked.

‘We don't know. He was found trying to crawl down the road to Helensburgh early this morning. No one has been able to get anything out of him. He was also suffering from hypothermia. He is in surgery and later will be transferred to the sickbay here if everything goes well.’ I wondered how on earth Barry would be trying to crawl down the road with two broken legs. I guess he was somewhere near Mae’s house and wondered if Mae's husband had sent someone round to ‘sort him out'. I didn’t understand why we were going the FOSM’s office. Did the Admiral want to see me? They say it’s an ill wind that blows nobody good. I followed Lt Lucas into the building reception. He conversed with the receptionist and afterwards came to me and we went up to the top floor in an elevator. The Admiral got up from his desk and came over to me.

'Hello Chief Clark.' he said in a rich baritone voice that could boom out on any parade ground - not that he would ever need to do that though. 'Very pleased to meet you.' He added extending his hand out. Somewhat bewildered I took his hand; a large hand, strong and warm. I said hello and he invited me to sit on a soft lounge chair by a small coffee table. A porcelain pot of coffee was there along with delicate coffee cups. 'Well Chief, we have a problem.' The admiral smiled at me 'But, maybe we have a solution. You have had some very serious allegations levelled at you and, if true, you will be facing a court martial where you will certainly lose your rate and with a possibility of being discharge from Her Majesty's Navy.' I was about to speak but he held up his large hand to stop me. 'Chief Petty Office Baldwin has met with some misfortune and will not be able to sail at the weekend when Submarine Messenger embarks for its first patrol.' He paused to let the obvious consequence of this to sink in. He then stated the obvious 'The Messenger cannot sail with only two Nuclear Chiefs of the Watch. Furthermore, it is too late to train someone new.' So, I guessed things were beginning to look up for me. 'Chief Clark, I have gone through all the paperwork associated with your incident ashore and have spoken at length with a Mr Gary Osbourne whom you have met.' I nodded focusing all my attention on this very senior man. 'The Police will not drop their case and unless your Lady friend comes forward things do not look very rosy for you.' He paused again studying my reaction. I was nervously rubbing my hands in my lap. 'I could issue an order for you to return to Messenger to complete this patrol, but your morale would be low. It is not good for a senior person, such as yourself, who has responsibility to many subordinate rates to have such a negative attitude. For me, I consider that because you were witnessed being collected by a lady, who you describe as the missing lady, in the stolen car and I believe this adds a considerable weight to your veracity. I cannot predict what the police will do but I can guarantee there will be no Court Martial afterwards.' The Admiral sat back in his chair with a satisfied posture. 'So, now, when I sign the order for you to return to your Submarine, I suspect your faith in the Naval Disciplinary Act will be restored.' I felt a big weight had been lifted from me. I could not stop the smile spreading across my face and my breath caught in throat. I feared I would burst out crying. I was overjoyed.

Lt Lucas and I went back to the Administration building where Lt Lucas authorised the return of my ID card and security pass. He informed the regulating staff that the status of House Arrest had been lifted. I was free.

There was no news of Barry. I would try to locate and communicate with him later. My first priority was to return to the Submarine and catch up with the progress on making ready for the coming patrol. I had to take control of the bar books again.

I discovered the Messenger would put to sea on Saturday. We had just two days. A directive had been issued, by Mr John Smith, that before we sailed all ID and security passes had to be submitted to the Cox'n and these would not be carried on the Submarine. We were not allowed to carry any material that would identify us; no personal letters, driving license or personal mementos. The only clothing we were allowed would be polyester overalls, socks and underclothes. Everything else would be locked in a store on the jetty and would be available to us when we returned.

I spoke with all the propulsion department and informed them I would be the duty NCOW, on Friday, and only needed one other senior rate and two junior rates. The rest could enjoy their last run ashore before we left. Pirate Jack Fox volunteered to be duty with me. I bumped into Lanky in the passageway on the accommodation deck. He mooched along with his head down and only grunted when I greeted him. Back to his normal self I considered.

I once again took charge of the bar books and checked the spirits store. I had several of these around the boat many of which were only known to me. The biggest was a blank breaker in the switchboard. I could quite easily store 12 cases of Bells whisky in there. I mainly drank Bells whisky so other spirits were in the main spirit store behind the bar. I made sure my locker had two full bottles and my flask was full. I decided it was time to see if I could get any news of Bonker. The sickbay told me he would be joining them later in the evening. I asked the duty Sick Bay Attendant to call me, in the senior rates mess, when Barry had arrived and was settled.

In the senior rates bar, I bumped into Jack Fox and we sat together. ‘All ready for tomorrow then Jack?'

‘As ready as I’ll ever be. Shame about Bonker; what the fuck did he do?’

‘Don't know but he broke his fucking legs doing it. Sickbay says he'll be here later on, so I’ll go and see him.’ Jack was silent a while then asked.

'What do you think about us not being able to take any personal gear on board. Bit fucking strong.'

'Well, I guess it's if we go down or get caught. I guess all that information would be useful to the enemy.'

'Fucking 'ell matey, do you think we might not come back then.'

'Well Jack, there were enough of our ships lost and men that didn't come back from the Falklands. It's all fucking war games.'

'Aye Chris, you're right matey. 'tis all fucking war games.' It's funny how Jack sounded more like a pirate the more beer he drank.

I got my call to the sick bay. 'See you tomorrow Jack.'

Barry was sitting up in his bed. His face was a pale grey and heavily lined. He had obviously suffered a great deal of pain. There was no joviality in his face, but his eyes sparkled when he saw me. 'Hey Barry, what the fucking hell happened?'

'Broke me fucking legs.' Barry spurted and almost broke out crying. His hands went to his head as if trying to stop it shaking. 'Honest Chris, I thought I was going to fucking die.'

'So, tell me. What happened.'

'Well, I was at Mae's house. We were up stairs getting amongst it when we heard a commotion downstairs. It was her husband. He somehow got into the house. He was shouting and smashing things about. Mae told me to hide. Fuck me Chris, Hide! I wanted to disappear! I was scared shitless man. Mae was pushing me away telling me to hide. She said he husband wouldn't hurt her. I went into one of the back bedrooms but there was nowhere to hide. I opened the window and thought I could reach the drain pipe. I could but...'

'Not close enough eh?'

'No. I almost got the fucker but couldn't get two hands on it so.....'

'So kerplunk.'

'Kerplunk is right. I heard a massive crack and pain shot up my back. I just laid there for a while and I could hear all the shouting upstairs in the house. I couldn't shout out for help. I was scared that cunt would come out. I found, if I sat, I could move backwards using my hands,' and he was demonstrating in his bed. 'I thought that if I could get to the road someone might stop for me.'

'What time was this then?'

'Oh, must be about one o'clock in the morning.'

'Fuck me man, I heard you were found around six.'

'Don't know. I got to their hedge and managed to squeeze through it. I kept passing out. I had to keep stopping to rest. Honest man, I thought I'd die.'

I pulled out my hip flask. 'Do you want a go with this?' I offered. He took it and took a good swallow and screwed up his face. He rested his head back on the raised pillow looking up to the ceiling. He took another swallow from my flask and gave it back to me.

'Cheers Chris. Fucking needed that.' We sat in silence for a while whilst I digested what he had told me. 'Remember some old lady trying to wake me up. I was out by the main road by now. Next thing I know I was being put in an ambulance and taken to hospital.' Barry was looking at me with a sad expression; so strange for Barry. 'Anyway, what happened to you. Last I heard you were in jail.'

I brought Barry up to date with what had happened to me since I last saw him. I told him that it was thanks to him that I got a guarantee from FOSM that I would not lose my rate.

'What happened on Sunday night after we left. Remember her old man was banging on the door.'

'Yeah. Mae called the police and they arrived fairly quickly. He calmed down a bit telling the police it was his house! Anyway, he left. The police spoke with Mae and suggested she apply for a restraining order. Can you believe it? Mae stood there talking to the copper in that see-through nightdress thing.' Barry was smiling now.

‘Yeah, I believe it.’

‘Mae said she liked Sally. She said she loved her accent and the 'coarseness' of her. She loved the fact she seemed to be uninhibited; as she herself is. She said she'd like us to get together again.

‘Good idea but Sally’s done a runner. No one knows where she is. Maybe she'll surface by the time I get back. What about Mae? Is she okay?’

‘Yeah. I spoke to her on the phone before I left hospital.’

‘Anyway mate, I’m going to fuck off. See you in three months.’ I stood up and turned to leave.

‘Hey!’ He stopped me. ‘Be good.’ The comment testified to the fact he had not lost his sense of humour.

Chapter 13

The Messenger Sails.

Friday morning, I arrived on board having had my normal breakfast in the Senior Rates Dining hall. 'Good morning Chief Clark.' Mr Smith greeted me politely. Mr Smith was always polite; always correct but, this was the first time he had greeted me in the morning.

'Good morning to you sir.' I replied good-humouredly and carried on through the control room.

I took my usual position in the mess and spread the bar books in front of me. The mess-man was busy cleaning the tables but stopped to pour me a pint of beer from the bar – he knew my routine. Tug and Ginge were huddled together and looked at me with suspicion as I entered. I nodded to them but said nothing. I considered them miserable fuckers. The beer had been delivered whilst I was away. It had been stowed in every nook and cranny available. I saw the delivery note and knew immediately there would not be enough for the whole trip. A lot of people wanted to abstain, whilst we were on patrol, but more would be in abstinence by the time we got back. No one would drink spirits; it was an unwritten rule. No one except me; I had my own stock. I accepted I needed alcohol. I had to have a 'fuzz' in my head. I didn't like to drink too much. I never liked being out of control and I didn't drink to pass out. I liked a good 'night-cap' to send me into a deep sleep. I accepted I would feel like shit when I woke up, but a quick shot of Bells would sort it out. I remember Mr Smith asking me, after I had first met him, if I had a drink problem. I told him I was the bar manager so could get a drink whenever I needed to. No, I didn't have a drink problem. I don't think Mr Smith appreciated the humour.

I went aft of the tunnel to see the state of the propulsion systems. Lanky was on watch and was chatting with his mate Dennis. Lanky looked up with an expression of horror on his face. 'It's okay Lanky. It's only me. I'm not going to lose me buttons so all's well.'

'Oh. That's good Chris.' There was no joy in his face.

'So, what's happening?'

'Not much. All water tanks full. All bilges empty. Shore supply steady. Battery on float. All self-analysis systems functioning correctly. No defects and no work in progress.' He gave the standard report.

'Okay Lanky. Thanks for that. I'll take over now. I think we'll start the reactor this afternoon and get some steam around the place. Flash up the TG's (Turbo Generator) and get rid of the shore supply. We'll leave the water pipes on until later and ensure all tanks are full.' I was now demonstrating my authority. 'Jack and I can take care of that, so you can piss off ashore. Go and get pissed for the last time. Bright-eyed and bushy-tailed for tomorrow morning though.'

'Okay Chris.' Alwyn replied not looking at me as he got up to leave.

'Lanky!' I called after him. 'Thanks for the couple of beers the other day. Really cheered me up.' Lanky just nodded at me and continued on has way fwd.

Alwyn Leonard was deeply disappointed to see me again. In his mind he knew I would be dead by Monday.

Of all the things that were about to happen on this Submarine my main interest was the little compartment at the far end of the aft escape compartment. I wanted to have access to this place when we went to sea. I perceived it to be a safe place where I could relax with a couple of glasses of Bells. I could tune in to any conversation I wanted to. I also considered I would be able to watch the movies being shown in the mess from there. That would give me three options: the one being shown in our mess, the one being shown in the junior rates mess or the one in the Wardroom.

I grabbed the log and flicked back through the entries of the last few days. I wanted to determine if Jake was still around. 'Hiya Chris.' I looked up. It was Jake. He had a broad smile across his face. 'Good to see you again.' he came towards me with his hand outstretched. I heard you had a bit of a problem ashore.'

I took his hand and shook it warmly. 'I was just thinking of you. I'm so glad you're still here I would hate for you to leave without me being able to say goodbye to you.'

'Same for me my old buddy.'

'So, when are you off then.'

'Tonight. Got a flight to London then tomorrow evening off to New York. Gives me a few hours to see some sights in London.'

'Come and have a beer in the mess before you go.'

'Sure thing.'

'Listen, is everything okay with all your systems.' I asked him seriously.

'Yeah. Everything fine. Just need to grab a few things and that's it. See you in the mess.' I gave him the thumbs up. 'About noon?'

'Wonderful. See you at twelve then mate.' So, my queries were answered.

It was a busy morning with lots of people coming and going. I told them of the program to start up the propulsion systems so there was a lot to prepare for.

Just before lunch time I went to the aft escape compartment to see if I could determine what would be needed to get into the

'Video' office. I knew a camera would be looking directly at this door, so I had to be seen not paying any attention to it at all. I walked past it the lifted the hatch to the lower level. My make-shift bed was still there so I gathered up all the rags into one, much neater pile. When I went back up through the hatch, I was able to scrutinise the fake door to the Video room. It seemed to me that it was secured with a standard padlock. The caged door front was the same as any other one on board, so it would be strange if this was locked by anything different. The front of all the store drawers were the fakes. I went back to the PCC thinking all I needed was that key.

I was already sat in my favourite position in the mess when Jake poked his head around the curtain. 'Come in Pal. Sit.' I indicated a seat for him as I got up to get him a beer. Jake was very concerned I had discovered the 'video' room and that I might not be able to keep his secret. I assured him I would say nothing. Jake could not impress upon me enough of doing this, as his career would be over if his superiors discovered he did not create the exclusion area effectively enough; he would be considered a security risk. I didn't want to concern him further by asking for the key. I could blackmail him for it, but I was genuinely fond of Jake and didn't want him to worry unnecessarily. So, I showed him concern that those cameras had recorded something of me that might cause me embarrassment. They may have seen me refilling my flask, at my locker or getting my head down in the aft escape compartment. Jake assured me that he had reset all the recording modules and they started again sometime yesterday. He also assured me the camera in the bunk space no longer has vision of my locker as we had moved it sometime before.

Jake was eager to go and get his things together for his trip. He was excited to see London. We said our farewells and away he went.

The afternoon was busy. We took the reactor critical and raised steam from the steam generators. The TG's were warmed through and run up and put on line. We then disconnected shore supply. We had a final filling up of the water tanks before the shore-connected hoses were disconnected. We started to warm through the main engines just to make a test of the steam systems. All was well with the propulsion systems of this new futuristic submarine. Similar tests and procedures were being carried out fwd. Electrolysers were started along with CO2 scrubbers. Air compressors and hydraulic pumps tested and put on line. Periscopes were raised and lowered. Jock Thames and Rees Jennings ran through a series of tests on the missile systems under the direction of Paul Wells. Missile hatches were opened and closed, and the tubes were vented and then re-purified. The gyroscopes of the missile guidance systems run up and full diagnostics checks were carried out on the launch systems.

By Friday evening things were beginning to settle down a little. Only the duty watch remained on board. I decided to try out the showers. As is normal, on a Submarine, a man will wash his undies and socks when he showers. He then will find a place where these can be hung to dry. It is not healthy for them to be hung in the bunk space. I knew exactly where mine would go. I put on a clean pair of overalls and marched off back aft with my wet washing in my hand. I had a length of cord in my pocket also. I stood on the deck plates by the hatch, to the lower level of the aft escape compartment, and selected locations to string up my washing line. I had to act naturally as I know I was being recorded. Once I was satisfied with my line, I hung out my underpants and socks. I adjusted them and was confident they blocked the line of sight, from the camera, to the video office. I then examined the padlock on the door and could not see any other impediment to the secret door opening if I was able to remove this securing.

To remove the lock was a very simple thing but it had to be replaced. I could get another padlock easily enough, but I could not put this in place if I was inside the room. The probability of anyone going so far aft is remote. The probability of someone going so far aft, when I was in the room, was even more remote and at the same time they would have to notice the lock was missing for me to be in danger. I didn't like it, but it seemed an acceptable risk.

Much later in the evening I went aft to take over the watch. The TGs were running so things were a little noisier, a little hotter and the familiar smell of warm lagging hung in the air. I took a walk around and again was amazed that no-one need be present in the TG room. I looked at the auto-watch-keeping panel and scanned all the parameters being monitored. Everything was in the green. I eventually made my way to the video room door and checked my washing still concealed the line of vision from the camera. I checked the hasp and it didn't seem very strong. Maybe I could modify it, so I could release the padlock as an option. Then I looked at the other side of the door and the hinges. These were only basic hinges and the hinge pin looked as if it could be pushed out. The pin was like a nail and the head prevented it dropping down out of position; gravity prevented it rising. I pushed it upwards; it moved easily. I did the same with the lower one and it too moved easily. I removed them both and found I could open the door in the other direction and gain entry. The inside looked the same as I last remembered it except the TV screen was dark. The chair also remained where Jake must have left it. The roller screen was pulled down over the controllers; I could not see any lock on this. I stepped inside and attempted to lift the screen and it moved easily. I was elated although I was full of fear, for some reason. My heart was skipping a beat. So, that was it. I wanted to explore more. I wanted to switch on the TV screen and scan round to see what I could see. However, I decided now was not the time. I needed more time and at a time when I should not be somewhere else. I replaced the door and dropped in the lynch pins. All looked normal. I felt sure I could pull the door closed, when I was inside, and no one would notice the pins missing. I was happy and feeling smug with myself.

Just after midnight Jack came and said he would now take over responsibility for the watch. Everything was just ticking along so nothing to worry about and nothing to do – just keep an eye on things. I told him I needed to collect my washing which gave me an excuse to go to the aft escape compartment. I quickly removed the lynch pins and entered the video room. I pulled the door shut and was confident no one would notice from the other side. I opened the screen door covering the controls to the cameras and switched on the TV screen which soon came to life and showed an image of the control room. A young junior rate was sitting close to the navigator's table. I surveyed the large dials in front of me. One, I knew, selected the camera. The others could select a time scale to look back upon. A day and time could be selected. I was not really bothered with this. I turned the selector control and a different image appeared on the screen. Many showed empty compartments and empty spaces. There were not too many people on board at the moment, so activity was light. I was beginning to feel confident with the controls and considering leaving for now when I saw Jock Thames in the torpedo compartment. He was sitting on one of the long benches in the centre of the compartment although he was talking to someone who was out of view. I could not find the head phones I had seen Jake use. I selected another camera and discovered who Jock was taking to. Tug Wilson and Paul Wells were working in the lower level of the torpedo compartment. I couldn't exactly see what they were doing but both were waving their arms around as if they were trying to explain something to each other. I decided I'd go and have a look later. I didn't want to spend too long here at this moment – Jack may come looking for me. I found the camera to the escape compartment door and checked no one was around. I turned off the TV monitor and pulled the screen cover down over the controllers. I decided I'd look for the head phones on my next visit. I secured the door and collected my clean washing and went to bed.

The next morning, when people started to come on board, I had assumed my normal position in the mess. The galley was functioning fully now, so I had breakfast with my beer. I prowled around the torpedo compartment, where I had seen Tug working but could see nothing of any interest. I did note the access hatch to the reserve fresh water tank was not fully secured. I re-entered the mess which was getting quite full now. Brian Wilson seemed to be in conversation with Paul Wells and Ginge Joe Green.

'Hey Tug.' I shouted across to him. 'I notice the hatch is not bolted down on the reserved fresh water tank.'

'No, it's not. There's no fucking water in it so it's okay.'

'Is there a problem with it then?' I asked.

'No. No, there's no fucking problem with it. In any case it's got fuck all to do with you.' Tug was being overly aggressive.

'Well, it's got a lot to do with me. If there is no problem, why is the hatch not secure. This is a fucking Submarine and it don't make sense for the hatch to be off.'

'Look. It's got fuck all to do with you. Get your fucking nose out of my business.' The rest of the mess descended into silence as this discussion suddenly became more heated.

'If there is nothing wrong with the tank why is the hatch off and why is it not full of water. Why take off the shore supply hoses when we have such a big fucking tank empty. When you finally get around to making the thing secure, I must use my men and machinery to make water to fill that fucking tank,' and I was pointing fwd as I said this. 'That's what it fucking has to do with me.' I had approached him now and was staring down at him. If this got physical, I was going to lose.

'Paul, go and secure the reserve fresh water tank hatch,' he said to Paul by his side without moving his eyes from mine. I returned to my seat and the mess returned to normal, as did my heart rate. I was pissed off. If that tank is not that important, I could have stowed beer barrels in it.

It was strange to see the entire crew wearing polyester overalls with no badges or name tallies. The Cox'n collected everyone's personal belonging: wallets, watches and jewelry along with ID cards and security passes. All items were listed and signed for and a receipt given. These would be held in a safe in the security cabin ashore and be waiting for us on our return.

Some strange civilians were seen moving around. They would be making final checks to the sophisticated sonar, listening and intelligence gathering devices we had on board. They soon disappeared as the time to depart was approaching. It would be normal to carry some 'passengers' but, it seemed automation had extended to their spy gear.

Harbour Stations were called on Saturday afternoon and we all prepared for departure. A total of 42 crew were on board including four officers and Mr John Smith. HMS/M Messenger silently eased away from the Jetty at Faslane and aligned itself with the Gare Loch and proceeded, under its own power, to commence its first mission.

The program was we would sail down the Gare Loch into the Clyde Estuary. We would make a surface passage to our diving area, which we would reach early on Sunday morning, somewhere North of Ireland and West of Scotland. We will then reach our diving location and send our diving signal; the last signal to be sent until we return some 90 days later. We will then submerge and proceed to our patrol area. A 'Clear Lower Deck' is planned for Sunday morning at 11:00. All ratings not on watch, and all Officers, will gather in the torpedo compartment to be addressed by the Captain. I guess we will be told of what is expected of us and any other bullshit he can think of to promote a high state of morale during an arduous, yet very important, mission.

Just before 03:45 on Sunday morning I went aft with my wet washing in my hand. I had the Morning watch – 04:00 to 08:00. I had a young CPO with me, his name was Terry, who would keep an eye on the mechanical systems. I also had a junior rate who would do whatever we told him to do. I told Terry I wanted him to keep a close eye on the steam systems of the TGs and the Main Engines. He soon disappeared down the machinery spaces. I told the JR to stay put in the PCC for a while, so I could check a few things out. I went aft with my washing, I hung this obscuring the offending camera before removing the lynch pins to the video room door. I went to the lower level and retrieved a big bundle of clean rags: enough to make a bed. I arranged myself in this special room. I turned it into my retreat. I could come here, watch some TV and get my head down to sleep off a drunken stupor; I had two bottles of Bells at the ready. I found the headphones in a drawer along with a list of all the camera location corresponding to the numbers on the dial. Once I was satisfied, I locked everything up and resumed my watch-keeping duties.

Just before 08:00 Lanky stepped through the aft tunnel door with his mate Dennis behind him. I handed over the watch to Lanky who scanned around the various panels and machinery. He seemed disinterested. I could muster no energy to try and chat with him. He was no longer the Lanky Leonard I used to run ashore with some years ago. As I was about to go, he asked me. 'What do you think about this trip Chris?' I thought for a while.

'What d'ya mean?'

‘Have you ever thought we might not come back?’ This seemed to be Alwyn at his morbid worst.

‘If we don’t come back, we don’t fucking come back. That’s life. No good worrying about it.’ I turned and went fwd for breakfast. Breakfast is always the best after a morning watch. I was glad to not see Brian Wilson in the mess; he had taken the watch in the control room with Paul Wells and their run-around Leading Stoker Tom Gill. Rees Jennings had assumed responsibility in the galley. Jock Thames would patrol around the machinery spaces as directed by Tug. Joe Green closed-up in the SONAR compartment. Mr John Smith smiled inwardly. ‘His’ crew was all in position. He had spoken with each of them recently giving the final details of the plan to take control of submarine Messenger. He was confident each one of them would be able to carry out their part of the scheme.

Breakfast consisted of fried egg, bacon, sausage, beans, tinned tomatoes and toast. The plate was loaded to the gunwales and I devoured the whole lot and washed it down with two pints of CSB. I knew it would be pointless to try and sleep in the bunk space. Diving stations would be called soon and then later ‘clear lower deck’. So, I decided to hide away, in my secret compartment, and have a few shots of Bells. I did just that. I was particularly tired because of my duty the day before and lack of sleep. I quickly spread out the rags, in my retreat, and with my belly full of breakfast, beer and Bells, I soon fell into a deep unconsciousness.

At 08:30, on Sunday morning, Diving stations were called. The

Messenger slowly lost buoyancy and sank beneath the waves to an environment it was designed to be in. The crew checked round for leaks and reported all was okay.

At 10:00 Tug told Jock Thames and Gilly Gill to go around and check no one was in the Junior Rates bunks space. Tug did the same for the senior rates. Tug was big enough and senior enough to drag anyone out of their bunks without opposition. Everyone had to be up and around for the Captain's address. At 10:45 another round of the bunks space was made to ensure no one had crept back in. Shortly afterwards there was a main ship's broadcast announcement telling all non-watch personnel to muster in the torpedo compartment for a Captain's address. Lanky called his Junior rate to the PCC. Taff Evans was in his mid-twenties. He too was divorced and so had a lot in common with Alwyn. Both were Welsh which added to the bond. 'Taff you got to go fwd and listen to the Captain.'

'Aw. Do I have to. It's only bullshit.'

'Yeah. You gotta go.'

'Okay.' And he turned to leave. Alwyn watched him disappear into the tunnel and close the door behind him.

Mr John Smith would remain in the control room during the Captain's address, but he slipped into the Wardroom bunk space to execute the next procedure of the plot.

There were two rows of benches, the length of the torpedo compartment, and either side of the centre line where the crew could sit and face each other. Many were smoking and chatting amongst themselves. The last few stepped through the hydraulic door and up the two steps to the upper level of the torpedo compartment. Tug stood by the door shouting orders urging everyone to hurry up and take their positions inside. The officers came all together led by Lt Lucas – the youngest man on board. The Captain was the last to step up. He said his thanks to Chief Wilson and smiled at him warmly. Tug had already moved the hydraulic door from its fully open position in preparation to closing it. He watched as the Captain made his way down the aisle, between the two crew-filled benches and saw the crew fall silent as their eyes followed the Captain's progress fwd. Tug reached up and retrieved two small canisters from the locker adjacent to the door. These were like grenades. In fact, they were smoke grenades as used for fire exercises. Tug pulled the pins and tossed them amongst the crew assembled in the compartment. He then moved the hydraulic door actuator to 'close' and the door swung towards him. As soon as the crew saw the smoke, they reached up for the Emergency Breathing System (EBS) masks. These were housed in two rows of lockers above each bench. As the doors opened the masks fell out and dangled in front of the crew who were now stirred into action. Almost all thought it was another exercise. Many similar exercises had been carried out in the last few weeks. The 'smoke' was actually a vapour but looked like smoke, it smelled like smoke and it had the same choking effect as smoke. Each member of the crew, including the Captain, grabbed an EBS mask and held to their faces, they clamped their teeth on the mouth piece and formed a seal with their lips around it. As soon as the demand valve felt the low pressure, of a breath intake, it would open and allow the fresh air to flow. This was not fresh air. The crew, within the torpedo compartment, did not know that the first breath of air from the mask would be their last.

Since Mr John Smith and Samir came to an agreement John had an incredible amount of power and authority. Samir was a powerful man in the ministry of defence. He appointed John as Head of Submarine Security so he could select the crew and his helpers. John could do many things without being questioned. He had personally ensured that the torpedo compartment had its own dedicated EBS. An extension to the pipework was routed up, through the deck, to the bunks space of the wardroom. It terminated in a quick release coupling in the bunk he occupied. From this position one could breathe the air from the torpedo compartment EBS but that was not why Mr Smith had designed it so.

When Mr Smith visited the Wardroom bunk space, before the Captains address, he took from his locker a gas cylinder about the size of a large, fat cucumber. This had a short rubber hose and a quick release connection identical to the EBS. John connected it to the system and opened the valve of the cylinder. There was a low hissing as the high-pressure gas rushed into the EBS and polluted the fresh, clean air. Samir had sent the cylinder to him. It contained a hybrid Sarin nerve gas code name Sarin B2. As soon as the gas was release from its high-pressure container it spread around its new environment. Each SarinB2 gas molecule needed to be as far apart from its neighbour as possible. With-in milliseconds the whole torpedo compartment EBS was contaminated with a homogeneous mixture of SarinB2. One normal breath of this mixture contains enough molecules to kill an entire army. However, SarinB2 breaks down rather quickly. Within about 3 hours the EBS air would be safe to breathe again.

When the SarinB2 molecules passed the demand valve of the EBS mask and entered the body they instantly attacked the central nervous system. The muscles, of the body would freeze, holding the body in the position it was when the last breath was taken. The heart would be stopped, and, after a few seconds, the brain would cease to work. When the brain died the muscles would relax and the bodies would collapse to their lowest state of energy.

Within seconds everyone in the torpedo compartment was dead.

Tug sauntered into the control room as if he was carrying a ton weight on his shoulders. 'Well done Brian.' John said to him. 'We knew it would happen. We chose to do it. Now it's done.'

'Yeah. It's fucking done now.'

Mr John Smith reached for the ships broadcast microphone and cradled it in his lap whilst he considered what he was going to say. 'Listen up there. The hardest part of our mission is now completed. When the smoke clears in the torpedo compartment we have to start disposing of the bodies. Well done everyone.' John pause then pressed the broadcast button again. 'I hope to rendezvous with our mother ship within the next day or two.'

John knew he had to get to his chosen ones to reassure them all will be okay, and this dreadful thing will soon be behind us.

'Hello Alwyn.' John greeted Lanky in the PCC. 'You okay?'

Alwyn looked up at John and could not see any sign of guilt or regret on his face. Alwyn felt terribly guilty. His biggest problem was that he sent Taff fwd. He sent Taff to his death. He knew he would have to put this behind him and see this thing through to the end.

'Yes. I suppose so.' Alwyn took a deep breath and seemed to accept what has happened has now been done so he had to move on to the next stage. 'When do you think this mother ship thing will be here?'

'Two days at the most. No more. We have to dispose of the bodies. It's part of the deal. They want a 'clean' submarine.'

'Yeah.' Alwyn was melancholy again. 'Tell me seriously are we going to end up dead? Will we get paid?'

'Don't worry Alwyn. You have already been paid. I pay all of you. I was recruited and paid to recruit you. I was given a brief and a big payment with the promise of more. I transferred a further one million pounds to the original bank you received the first payment.'

'So, what's to stop them not letting us get off the mother ship?'

'Well, the plan is that we all fly ashore in a helicopter. I have arranged for two hire cars to be available to us at Prestwick airport.'

'Yeah, but they could make the helicopter crash.'

'Alwyn, once I had agreed to do this job, I also had the same fears you have now. I was lucky to have a great deal of authority and so introduced start up codes which are built into all these systems. If you scram this reactor you will need a 'start up' code to take the thing critical again. The same with the TELSA systems, the missile systems, the torpedo systems and all the rocket systems. Some have a self destruct mechanism that if the wrong code is used then that particular system will burn up. I have all these codes in a book that I have hidden, in a safe place, somewhere in Prestwick Golf Course.' Alwyn was nodding approval on hearing this. 'I have informed my contact of this and agreed to meet him there when I will hand over the book once I see my money is in my bank. You see there will be nine of us. We will just look like visitors and the story is we are there to play golf. I cannot see us being massacred in a location such as Prestwick Golf Course.' Alwyn was assured by this explanation. It is clear more planning than he realised has gone into this. He had already submitted is driving license, passport and a small hold-all of clothes to John so he could see the plan working.

'Okay then John, let's hope everything goes to plan.'

'I think we have everything covered. Keep things steady.' John then made is way fwd.

John returned to the control room and mentioned Brian Wilson to follow him as he about turned and went down the ladder to the accommodation deck. Tug followed John and Tom Gill and Paul Wells followed behind. The torpedo compartment door loomed up before them. They were dreading what they would find on the other side. The beauty of using vapour smoke bombs is that after a short while the 'smoke' disperses; there is no need to ventilate. John peered through the inspection window in the door and announced it was okay to open the door. John pushed over the actuator and the door hissed open. The smell of the smoke grenades hit them, but the air was clear. The vision that greeted them was appalling. Thirty-two people were toppled down upon each other. Some still had masks on and their heads were held up by the connecting tube to the quick release connection. Others had their masks ripped off as they fell. All the faces seemed expressionless except for their eyes. Most had blank wide staring eyes– no one died in agony, only in surprise. Some had fallen backwards, and their legs were in the air and their torsos on the deck outside of the confines of the two benches. Most fell forward and collapsed in on each other. It was a tangled orgy of death. It reminded Tug of the pictures he had seen of the German concentration camp victims; all piled up, but these were not skin and bone. These were all fit and healthy human beings. Maybe they drank too much but that's not a great sin. John had selected these people as he had selected his special eight. He knew they would all die but there would be no grieving wife and the children were not small but to some extent immune to the pain of seeing their parents fight and separate, and then continue to fight. Now, these professional submariners, who once held comradeship and alliance, to one's fellow shipmate, above all else, were a problem. They had become victims of a few who sold their souls for the silver dollar. The deal was that they would be disposed of, before the submarine was handed over. 'Okay Tug. You know what to do. I'll send Rees and Raymond to give a hand.' John walked away and left them to it.

Tug was in charge in the Torpedo compartment. He told Gilly to make ready the stand pipe. The stand-pipe was the pipe-work John Smith had given Tug the responsibility of getting manufactured in the inboard workshop. Tug told Gilly to unbolt the inspection hatch of the reserve fresh water tank and cursed me at the same time for insisting it be fully bolted down.

The reserve fresh water tank was another addition Mr John Smith insisted upon before leaving Philadelphia. Submarine Messenger did no need a reserve fresh water tank. The normal fresh water tank held sufficient water for the needs of the crew. It needed to be topped up now and again, but it did not overburden the water making capacities of the evaporators. It was designed with a linking pipe to the fresh water tank, with the first section being reinforced rubber. This would be normal as it would not transmit vibration and hence noise. Another pipe went aft on the starboard side. There was another pipe, from the bottom of the tank which could be connected to the bilge pump. The inspection cover was overly large, and it took all the strength of Gilly to move it to the side. Paul removed the rubber pipe section and bolted the stand-pipe on the flange.

Rees mounted the two steps up to the deck level and felt sick. He was not a good sailor and we had just come to the end of a surface passage. Submarines are not the most comfortable sea going vessels on the surface. Rees leant against a torpedo whilst he composed himself. He was appalled at what he was looking at. He was appalled that he was part of this. He knew he had to pull himself together and steel himself to do the job he had agreed to. Jock bounced up the steps behind him then stood still as a statue 'Fuck me!' he murmured under his breath. Then aloud 'Oh, fuck me, fuck me. Fucking hell!' Rees looked at him with a pathetic expression on his face.

'Right you two.' Tug caught their attention. 'Let's get on with it. Rees get in there.'

Tug didn't say where he had to 'get in' but Rees knew. They had discussed this and planned it all. Everyone had their job to do. Rees had to get into the tank and when the bodies were dropped in, he had to drag them to the aft bulkhead of the tank, and 'stack' them. They needed to be laid out straight, so the minimum of space existed between them. Rees would have to do this on his knees due to the restriction of height inside the tank. This part of the job had to be done as soon as possible before rigor mortis set in and before too many bodily fluids would leak out of their dead shipmates. Jock Thames dragged the first body from the pile and he and Gilly manoeuvred it into the hatch opening. A dead Taff Evans flumped to the floor of the tank. Rees dragged him away from the opening, straightened him out and pushed him into position on the back wall of the tank. It was hard work, yet Taff was only a small man and Rees wondered if he would be able to deal with the bigger ones.

'That's the first fucker.' Jock announced matter-of-factly as he went back for the next body.

Mr Smith was checking things in the control room. Course and depth had been set and the Messenger would sail in a 'Box' pattern at a depth of 150 feet. The box was about five miles square. The sea depth was an average of 300 feet and the sea bed was sandy with few rocks. The Submarine was being controlled on auto pilot. Speed was set at eight knots. John inwardly complimented himself of his design.

Ginge was scanning his SONAR receivers when John poked his nose around the sound room door. 'Everything okay?' John asked.

'Everything's fine. We have a day or so before we expect to hear anything right?' John nodded. 'The only thing to worry about in this area is fishing boats but so far nothing.'

'Okay. Good. Let me know if anything changes.'

John didn't want to, but knew he must go to the torpedo compartment to see how things were progressing. He knew it was necessary to be seen to be involved with the bad things to keep his team focused.

Jock and Tug had got into a routine of dragging the bodies to the tank hatch and they both did this without the initial distaste for the job. Rees had pushed all the bodies to the extremes of the tank, and even piled them upon each other but was running out of space. He was able to stand up in the hatch opening and let the bodies drop on his thighs that he could use to direct them into a location away from the hatch. With five corpses left he climbed out of the tank. There was ample space left and the final quintet could lie where they fell. Ironically the final body was that of the Captain. 'Button that fucking hatch down.' Tug barked to no one in particular.

'Well done men.' John complimented them when the inspection cover was being bolted in position. 'How's the pipe-work Brian?'

'Good. No problems. I'm just going to make the connection in the electrolyser space and I'll be back.' Tug climbed up from the lower level and took a deep breath as he surveyed his surroundings. He noticed some mess on the deck-plates where the bodies had 'leaked'. There were traces of piss and some skid marks of squigey shit. 'Rees! Scrub this mess up will ya.' He noted that Jock had moved on to next part of the procedure.

In the electrolysers compartment Tug disconnected the Hydrogen inlet pipe to the pump which discharges this unwanted gas overboard, a by-product of the electrolyser process. He then connected the pipe from the Reserve Fresh Water tank to the pump inlet and started the pump. He returned to the torpedo compartment. Paul was dressed in a submarine escape suit. The hood was over his head, all zipped up, and he wore rubber gloves. Tug noticed the tank was secure and checked the pressure gauge on the outlet side of the stand pipe. The pump of the electrolyser had created a low pressure inside the tank. 'Okay, let's go then,' Tug ordered. Jock had been retrieving the acid containers from their stowage's. Tug dragged one towards him and removed the seal on the cap and then removed the lid. He pushed it towards Paul 'Be fucking careful.' He warned. Paul opened the valve at the base of the enlarged section of the stand-pipe. He then carefully lifted the acid container and gingerly poured the contents into the standpipe. The fluid ran smoothly. The low pressure, inside the tank, ensured there would be no toxic fumes drifting back into the submarine's atmosphere. 'Good.' Tug said as he saw the whole contents of the container transfer into the tank. John had calculated how much concentrated sulphuric acid would be needed to totally dissolve thirty-three dead bodies. He added ten percent to this and had them stored on board under the premise they were free issue with the battery. No one questioned this. He knew, with this amount of acid, all the bodies would be consumed within about three days. Meanwhile all the toxic gases, generated by the acidic degradation process, would be pumped into the sea.

Finally, the liquid slurry contents of the tank could be pumped out with the bilge pump, ditched overboard and the tank flushed out with fresh water. No trace would ever be found.

When all the acid bottles were empty Paul climbed out of his suit. He carefully turned it inside out as he did so, just in case any acid was on the outside. He was sweating and was relieved to be unencumbered. He ran his fingers through his hair and, somehow, felt very satisfied that he had done a good job. Rees had scrubbed the deck plates, got rid of the dirty water and was now taking a shower. Jock was returning the empty acid containers to their stowage's. Soon the torpedo compartment returned to normal. It was clean and tidy. All ready for sea. It is amazing to think that just a small few hours ago it was the venue of such a crime. A crime of such callous cowardice perpetrated for the sole purpose of money.

'Right.' Tug said. 'Let's all go and have a fucking beer. We have earned it.'

Chapter 14

The Escape

Somewhere, very far away, I heard the main broadcast summoning everyone, not on watch, to a Captain's address in the torpedo compartment. I was snuggled up on my bed of rags and just emerging from a deep, blissful sleep. I was in my special secret room. I was not going to disturb myself yet. I knew my head would hurt if I moved it. I decided not to move it. I was slowly coming back to reality but felt so comfortable I was going to savour these moments for a little longer.

I heard the main broadcast click in again. 'Listen up there,' it started. My interest was immediately roused. I recognised Mr John Smith's voice. Smith was only on board in an advisory capacity. Everyone accepted he was keeping an eye on the Captain who was relatively inexperienced. He should not be using the main broadcast to address the crew. He continued 'The hardest part of our mission is now completed.' What the fuck is this man on about! 'When the smoke clears in the torpedo compartment we have to start disposing of the bodies.' What? 'Well done everyone! I hope to rendezvous with our mother ship within a day or so.' What on earth is this man on about! He mentioned smoke in the Torpedo compartment which means we must have had a fire! Why did I not hear the alarm? My immediate response was to get up and find out what had happened. I wobbled a bit as I stood up, but I soon steadied myself. My mind skipped to the comment of 'disposing of the bodies' and meeting some mother ship. Something inside me flagged up caution. I did not need to rush off to find out what was going on. I had it all in front of me. I spun the dial round to one of the control room cameras. An empty control room was displayed on the screen. I selected other cameras in the control room, but they only revealed the same, an empty control room! I could not understand why the control room would be empty. We have just dived at the start of a long patrol. Smoke in the torpedo compartment flashed in my mind, so I selected the torpedo compartment camera. Sure enough, I could see smoke, but I could make out some shapes. Nothing seemed familiar. I would come back to this. I decided to check the PCC. On the screen appeared Mr John Smith chatting with Lanky Leonard. I quickly grabbed the ear phones and planted them on my head and clamped the cans to my ears. I could not believe what I was hearing. Lanky Leonard was paid one million pounds! I heard Lanky asking about the mother ship; John had mentioned this in his broadcast. Next, they talked about going ashore to a golf course and John handing over a book of codes to someone. At this stage I didn't know what was going on. My heart began to beat overtime. I was beginning to be very frightened. I flicked the dial back to the torpedo compartment. The smoke was clearing, and I was looking at a pile of dead people. Was I really looking at a pile of dead bodies? It was a grotesque sight. I felt light-headed and feared I would pass out. I began to shake when I realised I should probably be with them. I changed the cameras and viewed this terrible scene from a different angle. My eyes were riveted to this heap of inert bodies - some I could instantly recognise. As I was switching from one camera to the next, I saw the door begin to open. Mr John Smith entered and climbed up the two steps and looked upon the pile of deceased humanity. I noticed he had no expression on his face. Tug followed, then Paul Wells, and then Tom Gill. Oh my God, I thought to myself. Oh my good God. I didn't know what to do. I knew they must never know I am here else I would be thrown on top of the heap and be the last to die. So much was going through my mind. I suddenly realised why Lanky was so off with me. That bastard knew I would die! And that's why he was so pleased to see me inboard when he thought I was going to lose my rate. Checking the screen again I could see Jock and Rees had joined the others in the torpedo room. I wondered how many were involved with all this. Then my mind tried to analyse why this had happened. I didn't understand what 'the mother-ship' would be. It was clear the people, who were still walking around, were planning to be landed ashore. John told Lanky there would be nine of them posing as golfers. That must mean there are nine people involved in this scenario.

I watched in horror as the bodies were dragged away and dumped in the Reserve Fresh Water tank. Just about when I thought I could not be more horrified or appalled I see the containers of battery acid being dragged out and tipped into the tank.

I moved the dial back to the PCC and Lanky was chatting with Dennis. Lanky seemed to be filling Dennis in with what Smith had told him. 'We have already been paid our next million,' Lanky told him 'John said he transferred it before we sailed.' Dennis looked surprised and also pleased.

'Oh, that's good then. I was beginning to think we wouldn't get it.'

'Apparently Smithy pays us, and he gets paid by whoever started all this thing off.'

'You're having a boat built aint ya Lanky.'

'Yeah. It's all done now. I went down a couple of weeks ago for the final inspection. It's fucking beautiful.'

'I'm having one built in Miami. All kitted out with diving gear for treasure hunting. Trouble is it's not in my name. I couldn't give 'em any ID. Well I could but didn't want to use my name.'

'Wouldn't they let you use a code?'

'A code? What the fuck's that?'

'Well,' Alwyn started to explain 'When I told the boat builders, I wanted to remain anonymous, I gave them the name Owen Jones. I wanted to be more Welsh' he was smiling now. 'They said if I couldn't give them identification, I had to give them a code which would be unique to me so that would be my ID.'

'Ah. So, what did you do? Give them your date of birth?'

'Nah, has to have some letters.'

'Like your official number or something?'

'Well it could be, but other people would know that. They told me some people use their car registration. I aint got no car so gave them my old beer number from when I was on Valiant. We were drinking more beer then than the Ark Royal so hardly ever likely to forget that. So how did you get yours built?'

'My diving partner lives in Bimini and is an American citizen so it's in his name.'

'So, you pay and it's his boat. Sounds a bit dodgy to me.'

'No, we have a contract.' Dennis didn't like the way Alwyn grunted. 'Where is your boat then?'

'It's in a storage facility Princes Boat Storage next to where it was built. They said they would store it for six weeks free of charge. As soon as we get ashore, I'm off. I withdrew all my money and stored it on board.'

'Really how did you do that?' Dennis asked with real interest.

'I went to one of the big banks in Glasgow, an English bank. I asked them to give me a statement. The balance was £525,000. and they asked me if I wanted to make a withdrawal or transfer. I didn't really but thought what the fuck. I said I wanted to withdraw the whole lot. You should have seen his face. Anyway, he said I could but would have to wait. I told him I wanted to get the cash from a branch in Poole, so he arranged it. I went when I last saw the boat. I told them I wanted to leave some stuff on board. I turned up at the bank with my pusser's case, with a pusser's grip inside. Both were crammed pack with cash. Fucking heavy mate. Left them on board and the boat was taken to the storage yard. Still in the water ready to go.'

'Why did you do that? Surely its safer in a bank?' Dennis asked.

'I guess so, but I don't know where I'm going. I don't want to be running to the bank all the fucking time and what happens if I go to some backward place where they don't have proper banks. I still need money.'

'Good idea but mine's staying in the bank.'

An interesting conversation, and I was amazed they could talk so calmly after having been part of such a massacre. Anyway, there was still too much going on that I didn't know about.

I spun the dial again but found no-one in any of the messes. The control room was still empty, and Ginge Joe Green was in the sound room, with his head phones on, concentrating on the instruments in front of him.

I observed the torpedo compartment again. Rees was scrubbing the deck-plates and Jock was stowing the empty acid containers. Now I know why the fuckers weren't off-loaded when I requested it.

The torpedo compartment looked normal again. It was clear some careful planning had gone into this and, so far it seemed, it had been carried out with precision. The problem was I didn't know what the final goal was, and it was difficult for me to know what I should do let alone what I could do. One thing was for certain, I could not let these people know I was still around.

I heard Tug congratulate his 'team' and invite them for a beer adding that they deserved it! I wish I could have a beer that's for sure. I looked at the bottle next to me I knew I must keep a clear head. Whisky would not help. I lifted the bottle to my lips and took a big swallow anyway.

I selected a senior rates mess camera and watched as Tug poured beer for himself, Paul, Gilly and three more pints he placed on a table. Jock breezed in as if he owned the place and picked up a beer that Tug offered him. I now remembered seeing him in the Helensburgh Golf Club and understand how he qualified to be there and how he could afford to be a member let alone pay the bribe to climb the membership waiting list. Nobody was saying much. Mr Smith came in and took the beer offered to him. Shortly afterwards Rees entered with a tray full of food. He left and returned with another one. A pile of plates was placed on the table and everything was set for a party. A few seconds later Lanky walked in, surveyed the situation, then poured himself a beer. I suspected Dennis stayed back aft to look after things and Ginge would still be in the sound room.

I found it amazing that these people could act as if nothing had happened. They had just murdered thirty-two people and virtually disposed of their bodies and here they were carrying on as normal.

'You know something Tug?' Jock asked, 'I'm fucking sure I only counted thirty-two bodies.' Everyone turned to look at Jock

'Seriously, I was counting just to take my mind off what I was doing, and I only got to thirty-two.'

'You sure?'

'Well, I know people think I'm fucking thick, but I can fucking count.'

Tug ordered Paul to search the submarine from one end to the other. Tug was convinced Jock had made a mistake but felt obliged to check. I knew no one would find me here. A few minutes later Lanky came into the compartment and strolled around the upper deck plates only. That was the extent of his search.

The rest settled down to their beer. I heard Tug ask John a question. 'John, I'm a bit confused as to how the mother-ship will pick us up. You say it has doors in its hull that will retract, and we just surface up into it and tie up as if we were alongside.'

'Well, Brian that's about it.'

'But, the thing that concerns me, is, that we will be travelling forward, being driven by our main engines and we position ourselves under this, so called-mother ship,'

'That's correct.' John confirmed.

'Yeah, that's the easy bit. But when we surface into its hold, for want of a better word, the water in the hold will be static, relative to the ship. And if we are still under-way, surely we will crash into the fwd end of the hold.'

'You are right. First, we raise the periscope, so we can see what is happen. As soon as our conning tower breaks water, inside the hull of the mother-ship, it will be 'lassoed' with a specially made harness. This harness will be anchored fore and aft, with mooring ropes, and will also have mooring ropes port and starboard. All these four mooring ropes will hold the conning tower and winches will position us in exactly the right position. We then cut engines and blow main ballast.' John sat back triumphantly. Tug was nodding and nodding around at the others who all had the same concerns.

I must admit I was also impressed with John's explanation. Not only that it was clear to me the plan was to steal this submarine. I came out in goose pimples at the thought of it. They are going to steal this fucking submarine!

So, what the fuck do I do? I could stay on board, but I guess I would not be welcome on the mother-ship. The mother-ship must be some sort of super tanker. I can imagine there are enough super tankers sailing around the oceans; none raise any suspicions. I had to admit it seemed a good plan. Not only that, no-one in the UK is expecting to hear from us for at least 90 days when we send our surface signal. So, they have at least 90 days to get away before anyone comes looking. No, staying on board is not an option. I could leave. That would be easy enough. I could shut the aft escape compartment door and secure it on the inside so no one can come in. Then I just go out through the escape tower. Simple enough. I would need to know how fast we are going and how deep we are. My guess is we are just poodling around at about 100 and something feet - no more than 200 at most.

John said the we would rendezvous with the mother-ship in a day or so. Therefore, I have a little time - but not much.

Now, I must think about this. If I escape, then they still steal the submarine. And those bastards in the senior rates mess, who are drinking beer they have not paid for, will still get away with another million quid each. Trouble is I could not go out of this small room and arrest them and tie them up. Tug is a big man. Lanky is a big man. They would make mincemeat out of me.

No, I cannot overpower these people. But I can disable the submarine. Now, if I could escape and disable the submarine then that could be the best solution, all things considered. I took another long swig of Bells and felt pleased with myself that I had the beginnings of a plan. However, is this just a selfish plan. Am I just thinking of me. If I disable the submarine it doesn't mean that they can still not steal it. How would I disable it without destroying it. It would be no good me walking ashore and telling the Admiralty that I thwarted a gang of thieves stealing our submarine. Well done, they will say - where is it. Bottom of the fucking ocean would not be a good answer.

I looked at the TV screen and the party was progressing well. The group were laughing and joking and telling each other what they will do with their fortune. They had all spent a great deal of money it was clear. It made me angry that they can commit such a crime and then, so very soon afterwards, act as if the patrol is over. Well, I suppose for them it is.

I knew I had to act. If I stayed here for long I would need food and water. I could not go fwd. and get it and I could not ask anyone to bring it to me. I really could not leave the aft escape compartment. No one hardly ever visited this compartment, under normal conditions, and it would be less likely that there would be any visitors now. I knew there are lockers in this compartment with emergency rations in them. There should be enough rations for the whole crew because the whole crew could fit into, and escape, from this compartment and they may have to wait before they made their escape. Okay, so I should go out and investigate that. Thinking forward again. There are no toilets back here. If I stayed I would have to find somewhere to piss. I could not piss in the bilge because if the bilge alarm went off someone would come back here to investigate; mind you, I could remove the float from the bilge alarm then it would never sound. I certainly couldn't crap back here. Shit stinks and it would waft fwd. and if it got to the PCC then, again, they'd come back to investigate. So, I would have to move quickly.

I looked around me at this equipment. The two cassettes by my right foot had recorded everything that had occurred on this submarine since Jake reset it earlier in the week. Jake also told me that this is immediately transmitted should any transmission, radio or radar, be emitted by the Messenger. That's not likely to happen inside a super tanker. God knows where the messenger will end up and it may be so far in the future when any signal is transmitted - if ever - that they will not see the new owners. The recordings are overwritten after 100 days. It will give no details of how it got into their hands. They could rip out the radio gear and radar gear and replace it with their own and so no transmission will ever take place. I decided, when I make my escape, I will take one of those cassettes with me. At least I'll have something to show the Admiralty and there will still be one here doing its job.

I concluded what I should do. I had to leave this secret room and get some water from the emergency rations. I knew drinking so much whisky was not a good idea given my present situation. It would be better to put some water in it.

I had to take a look at the escape tower and familiarise myself with all of its element. All submariners are trained in escaping from submarines and must pass a practical test for doing so. A submarine escape compartment is part of the submarine training school at HMS Dolphin in Gosport. Above this compartment is a tower containing a column of water 100 feet high. From the escape compartment we enter the escape tower, shut the hatch we came in, and flood the tower. When it pressurises, the outer hatch opens and up we go. We must repeat this qualification every three years. Submariners look forward to this re-qualification. It means a few days in Dolphin when you can look up some old friends and have a fucking good run ashore. During the day you attend the lectures, talk through the procedures, and then do it for real - once with the survival suit and once with just a life jacket. It's good fun and no-one takes it too seriously. Well, I am just about to find out how well I absorbed the information.

I can make all the preparations. Get the suit ready and maybe find some old clothes amongst these rags. It's bound to be cold on the surface. Just before I go, I'll go through into the upper level of the Engine Room where the instrumentation racks are for the reactor.

I'll unscrew a couple of modules and steal myself to withdraw them quickly and return to the escape compartment shutting the door behind me. As I withdraw the racks the reactor will 'scram'. The Hafnium control rods will be released and plunge into the reactor core absorbing all the fission making neutrons. The reactor will shut down. Limited steam for TGs and main engines will be available. The watch-keeper will panic when the alarm goes off; he will not know immediately what to do. At some time, he will come back to check the instrumentation racks and discover some missing. Instantly he will know two things. One; the reactor cannot be restarted. Two; some other fucker's on board.

Now that sounds like a good plan. The submarine would not be 'disabled' it would just be wounded. It could still be recovered by their mother-ship. However, it would give me plenty of time to make my escape and the submarine would be slowing down and also reducing depth which is to my advantage. Once the reactor scram alarm goes off, I have to move quickly before any measures could be taken to disable me. I don't know what they would be but best not allow them any opportunity.

So, now time to move. I checked the TV. Dennis was still in the PCC and the party was still going on in the Senior rates mess. I eased the door open and squeezed through. I looked at the lockers containing the emergence rations. A note on the door informed me the locker contained 12 emergency ration packs. Another locker housed 12 litres of fresh water in half litre plastic containers. The locker doors were secured with a quick release catch held closed by bright-red fluorescent adhesive tape. I pulled off the tape and loaded myself up with water and packets of dried rations. I placed these in my room and went to examine the escape tower. I identified the flood valve, drain valve and vent. A hand wheel was there to close the upper hatch once someone had passed through it. This didn't bother me - I would be the last man and if the hatch was left open then it didn't matter. In fact, it gave me another idea. I opened the lower hatch and looked inside. Just like Dolphin I thought. I climbed in and stood with my feet either side of the open hatch. I looked up and decided to unlock the upper hatch. The hand-wheel moved surprisingly easily. I rotated it until it would rotate no more. The upper hatch was now unlocked. It remained shut due to the pressure of water acting down upon it. I looked at the vent tube - an open-ended tube ending just before the top of the tower. In Dolphin this ends much lower. When the tower is being flooded, and the water level reaches the end of this tube, it cascades down its inside and splashes out in the compartment below. The man below will shut the vent and the tower begins to pressurise as the level of water rises. Time to blow against a blocked nose to equalise the inner ear against the outside pressure. Failure to do this will fuck your eardrums up. The shorter tube, at Dolphin gives a longer time for the pressure to come on. The last man has a cap to block this tube from the inside of the tower. I looked at the flood valve and the tube that lets the flood water into the tower. The diameter of the flood tube was twice that of the vent tube. I opened up the air to the suit inflation station. I pushed in the diaphragm and air hissed out. Okay, I can do this. I climbed down out of the tower.

I also remembered the Submarine Lost buoy. This is a buoy that can be release from within the escape compartment. It will then float to the surface and start transmitting a signal that can be picked up by anyone with marine radio. It transmits details of the submarine and so it's location can be found. The buoy is tethered to the submarine with a cord of about 1000 meters. I would release this buoy just before I make my escape. To do so sooner would alert Mr Smith's men and so draw attention to myself.

It was that simple. How could it be that simple, but it seemed it was. I pulled out one of the escape suits from its locker and let it roll open. A smell of rubber filled my nostrils. A white powder covered my hands as I straightened the garment out. Inside it was the 'nappy'. It was literally that. A thick nappy made of absorbent gauze material which would soak up your piss if you had to spend a long time on the surface before being picked up. Apparently piss sloshing about your back is not good for your kidneys. I laid them to the side ready. Everything seemed to be moving so fast. Only half an hour ago I had no idea what I should do; now I was on the verge of executing my plan. I had given no thought of what would happen when I hit the surface. I would find that out when I got there.

I decided I would not put the cap on the vent pipe. The amount of water coming in through a two-inch pipe would be twice as much as that flowing out through the one-inch vent pipe. The tower would pressurise, albeit taking a greater time, which would be advantageous. The outer hatch would still spring open and away I would go. Water would continue to pour into the submarine via the vent pipe and open hatch. Before too long the aft escape compartment would flood. Now that will fuck Mr Smith, and his cronies, up.

If I do this now, I am sure there is not deep water beneath us. We only reached our diving area earlier. If the submarine sank, it could sit on the bottom and divers could retrieve it. There is not too much equipment, in the aft escape compartment, that would be destroyed by the sea water - except, of course, the stuff in the small room that nobody knows about.

I felt quite good about my plan. I don't know what Mr Smith and his crew would do. Best thing for them would be to escape from the fwd escape tower and hope the mother-ship picks them up. Mind you they would not want them. The fucking mother-ship wants this submarine, but it will be on the sea bed. And the coast guard, and Navy will be homing in on the Sub-Lost buoy.

Before I donned my suit, there were a couple of other things to prepare for. I had to make sure no one could open the Aft Escape Compartment door once I had shut it. Once the door is closed, with its hydraulics, a hand-wheel can be used to lock it in that position. I took the hand-wheel off from the Engine Room side of the door. I took the Engine Room-side hydraulic actuating lever off the control valve. I would also wedge a wheel spanner in the mechanism on the inside once I had shut the door.

I took the locking wire off the release handle of the 'Submarine Lost' buoy. I went back to the TV screen to check where the people were. Dennis seemed to be asleep in the PCC. The party was ongoing although Mr Smith was not with them. Paul was with them having finished his search. I flicked the selector round. I found John sitting at the Navigators table in the control room. Ginge was still in the sound room. He had a pint of beer in front of him.

I drank some water but not too much. I took a swig of whisky. I crept out into the Engine Room area and released the retaining screw, on two of the reactor instrumentation power supply units, ready for me to withdraw them.

For me, things were moving too quickly. Things had to move quickly I accepted that, but I had to be in control of these things. I was frightened I had not covered every angle. I went back to my room and didn't even bother closing the door. I ripped open one of the emergency ration packs and munched on some ships' biscuits. Ships' biscuits are the foulest biscuits in the whole wide world; they are rock hard and taste of compressed sawdust but... they are nutritious. I drank some water and some whisky. I knew I could withdraw the reactor instrumentation power supply units and get back into the escape compartment without being caught. I even felt supremely confident I could make my getaway from the escape tower. What now worried me was what I would find then. I would be in the middle of the ocean bobbing up and down on the waves. It would be cold, and I would soon feel sea-sick for sure. If I stayed on board I would die for certain. I was convinced of that. If I left, I may still die. I asked myself, what is better, stay here, drink my whisky and die or leave and die cold and bursting for a fucking drink. I knew I had to take my chances out of this submarine, and I also knew I had to do the best I could to stop this submarine from being stolen. I had already convinced myself I would leave the vent tube open which would eventually flood the escape compartment. I also decided to isolate the air to the after-most ballast tanks and so prevent them from being blown. Once this compartment was flooded there was only one way to go for the boat - and that was down. I was sure we were still in comparatively shallow water, so the submarine could be recovered. Mr Smith, and his crew, would have to decide what they would do. I accepted they may die. So what. They had killed the rest of the crew. If I survived, I could handle that guilt. The bottle of Bells was empty. I took a new one, I also withdrew one of the large cassettes from its rack and left my room. I was on the move.

I didn't know if it was better for me to dress up in my escape suit first, so I could get out quickly after pulling out the control power supply modules. Finally, I decided not to. I did not want to be encumbered in my movements or have the risk of being snagged up on the many protrusions that I may encounter. I would need more time, after the reactor scram, but I would have enough time to firmly secure the door and so I would be safe.

I was really scared. I was shaking but knew what I had to do. I took another big swig of whisky and before it hit my belly, I went up the step, to the upper Level Engine Room, skirted the corner of the racks and stood squarely in front of the two modules I was going to remove. I curled my fingers around the handles - one in each hand and tugged hard and straight. They both came out together. I heard the alarms go off in the PCC and I walked quickly and carefully back into the escape compartment. I remember gently placing the modules on top of a tool locker; careful not to damage them. I shut the door, locked it with the hand wheel and jammed in a wheel spanner so it could not be moved. I was now isolated in the aft escape compartment. I took the memory module and placed it on the small of my back and strapped it there using masking tape, wrapping it several times around my waist. I stepped into the nappy and secured the straps. I kicked off my boots and stepped into the survival suit pulling the hood over my head. I was about to climb into the tower when I remembered the buoy. I yanked the handle and it went slack in my hand - I guessed the buoy had gone but I could hear nothing. I climbed into the tower and put the lower hatch in place. I had already released the top hatch but checked it again. I had the bottle of

Bells with me and took another long drink from it. I screwed on the top and dropped the bottle inside my suit and then zipped up the hood. I pushed the air feed tube, that ran down the right-hand sleeve of the suit, into its socket and the suit inflated with a loud hissing sound. I opened the flood valve and then immediately took a firm grip of the ladder with my left hand. I knew as the water level rose, I would become buoyant and float towards the upper hatch. At Dolphin you wear a belt with a quick release catch. There is a diver in the tower with you and he connects this to the ladder to prevent you rising against the top hatch. When the tower is flooded, and the pressure is equalised you must indicate to the diver you are okay. He will then release the coupling and allow you to exit the tower. There is another diver who will catch you and he takes the same quick release catch and connects it to a central wire that is strung in the centre of the tank and runs its entire length. This ensures you rise without banging into the sides of the tank.

I had no diver with me. I watched the water rise and saw it pass the transparent screen of the hood. I could not see when it reached the top of the vent tube - it didn't matter; I was not going to cover the tube with a cap. I started to blow out through my nose against the nose clamp in anticipation of the pressure coming on. I hooked my foot under the lower rung of the ladder to keep me in position then I felt the impact of the water, from outside dropping in on me. The hatch had opened, and I let go of everything. I rose like a rocket and felt a tremendous bang on my skull. The last I remember was my body contorting and cracking of bones

Chapter 15

The Sinking

Dennis Warr was roused from his dozing by the clang, clang clanging of an Alarm. He opened his eyes and looked about him. It took him a while to realise where he was. The reactor panel was ablaze with red flashing lights, and the indicators on the electrical panel were doing a dance. He saw the mimic panel of the reactor instrumentation panel had only one line of instrumentation. He realised the reactor had 'Scrammed'. The reactor had shut itself down because two channels of instrumentation were lost. He stood back and watched as the steam to one TG was shut off. The indicators showed him the supplies were being restored, from the other TG and that its load was being transferred to the battery. Likewise, engine revs were reduced to a minimum. The automatic systems had taken over and reduced the steam take off and so reduced the load on the reactor. The reactor could supply no load. The reactor was shut-down. The telephone rang and Dennis snatched it up. 'What the fuck's happened?' Lanky demanded.

'Don't fucking know. We lost two reactor instrumentation supplies.'

'Go and fucking check it. I'll be right there.' and the line went dead.

Dennis cautiously went around to the cabinets on the upper level of the Engine Room. He didn't know what he was looking for, but he guessed he would see red lights on the offending modules. When he saw two blank holes he was horrified. His jaw dropped. All he could think was it was impossible. He returned to the PCC just as Lanky arrived closely followed by Mr Smith. 'So?' Lanky enquired holding his hands out questioningly.

'There's two modules missing.' Dennis informed him unconvincingly.

'What?' Then Lanky took off to see for himself. He too was horrified. He rushed past Mr Smith as he made his way back to the PCC. Mr Smith looked at the two empty slots. Mr Smith went aft. He knew someone must have taken these. He had confidence it would not be Dennis. Mr Smith was surprised to see the aft escape compartment door shut. Not only that, the hydraulic actuator was missing so he could not attempt to open it. He returned to the PCC.

'The aft escape compartment door is shut.' He said to Alwyn calmly 'Get it open will you please.'

Immediately Mr Smith went to the sound room. 'Joe? Anything?' he asked.

'No John, nothing. What's happened back aft?'

'Someone's scrammed the reactor and locked themselves in the aft escape compartment.'

'Who? For fuck sake, did we miss someone?

'Well, Jock said he only counted 32 bodies, but no-one believed him.'

'So, what do we do now?' Ginge asked but could see John was not paying him any attention.

'Let me know immediately if anything happens.' As he passed through the control room Tug was there with Paul Bomber Wells. 'Please come with me.' They followed him back to the PCC. 'Listen up. Alwyn, use the steam to safely cool the reactor and then put it in Emergency cooling. Brian, go and get the main motor ready; we have to go into battery drive. The battery should last a couple of days but be prepared to run the diesels to recharge the batteries. This little incident should not upset our plans. The mother-ship will be here soon, so everything should be okay.'

Everyone nodded, and Tug and Paul took off fwd. Dennis had removed the hydraulic actuator from the aft tunnel door and, also the hand-wheel, and was making his way to the after-escape compartment. Meanwhile Jock was cleaning up the aftermath of their lunch and Rees was dealing with the empty cooking pans and dirty plates. They were oblivious to their situation.

John watched Dennis fit the tunnel door actuator and hand-wheel to the aft escape compartment door. However, he was not able to open the door; the wheel spanner, on the other side, was doing its job. They all took turns to look through the small inspection window in the door, but nothing could be seen. Meanwhile I was strapping the recording cassette to my back and obviously out of the line of sight.

Dennis and John returned to the PCC and watched Alwyn adjust the load of the TG and he was monitoring steam temperatures and pressures along with the reactor temperatures. Should the cool-down rates be exceeded alarms will be sounded. The telephone rang. John answered it. 'John! Some fuckers released the 'Submarine Lost' buoy!' Ginge was panicking. There was silence while John digested this information. 'John! Did you hear!'

'Yes Joe, I got it. Thanks for letting me know.' John didn't say anything to Alwyn. He didn't want him to panic. John again went aft and peered through the inspection window. He could just see a pair of legs, dressed in an escape suit, disappear into the escape tower. John's heart sank. This was a game changer. He knew the buoy would be calling for help, and help would arrive. He doubted if they would have enough time to get safely into the hold of their saviour - the mothership. John just arrived in the PCC when the phone rang again. He knew Ginge was about to tell him someone had escaped. 'Yes Joe. I know,' he said before Joe could speak.

John quickly returned to the control room and snatched up the main broadcast microphone and held it to his lips. He thought for a moment and then depressed the activation button. 'Listen up everyone. We have a small incident. We had a saboteur on board who disabled our reactor. He has now left the submarine via the after-escape tower. We must surface to recover the 'Submarine Lost' Buoy which he released before his departure. Prepare to come to periscope depth.' The broadcast went silent.

'Fucking told you there was one missing.' Jock told Rees.

Brian Wilson, Tom Gilly and Paul Bomber Wells all arrived in the control room with wide eyes of fear on their faces. 'Listen men.' Mr Smith addressed them. 'The buoy is connected with a cord of at least 1000 meters. We have to recover the buoy. To just cut the cord is not good enough as the buoy will continue to transmit. I plan to get to periscope depth and locate the buoy and manoeuvre as close as possible to it. We can then surface and deal with it. We will not be able to bring the buoy down the submarine, it is too big, so we have to destroy it, or at least destroy the transmitter.' The three, in front of him were horrified to learn of this, yet nodded in acknowledgement to his plan. 'In the meantime, lets turn about,' Tug sat down at the control panel and switched off the auto control and took charge of the helm. 'Maybe we can get hold of our saboteur and deal with him.' John hissed.

Mr Smith went back to the PCC and informed Dennis and Alwyn of the events. Both were deflated to hear such bad news but reassured to hear there was a plan. 'Alwyn, I need you to get into a wet suit ready to leave through the conning tower - I want to stay as submerged as possible.'

'Why fucking me?' Alwyn asked with indignation.

'You were a ships diver at one time. You are a strong swimmer and a big powerful man. These are the qualities we need for this job.' John saw Alwyn accept this argument. 'I suggest you take

Thomas Gill with you. He's also a strong young man.'

Back in the control room John told Tug to steam in a tight circle. Fortunately, he had just completed the transition to main battery drive so could concentrate on these manoeuvres. The plan was to minimise the distance between the buoy and the boat. Once a visual contact had been made Messenger could reduce depth to ensure the conning tower was safely out of the water before the hatch was opened. Main ballast tanks would have to be partially blown to obtain the correct neutral buoyancy whilst some of the submarine was out of the water. This was not an easy manoeuvre so great care had to be exercised.

Submarine Messenger is also equipped with an automatic trim system. The system consists of two tanks, one in the torpedo compartment and the other in the aft escape compartment. Water can be pumped from one to the other to correct for trim. In the automatic mode this system is linked in the hydroplane controls. Should, for instance the bow of the submarine become heavy, water can be pumped from the fwd tank to the aft one or the hydroplanes could be angled to raise the front end. A combination of these actions is required for full automation, and is dependent upon overall buoyancy of the submarine. Tug noticed the fwd trim tank was full and the after one empty. This made the front end heavy, so the planes were angled a few degrees of rise. He noticed also the after planes were angled to rise. 'Back end is heavy sir.' Tug reported to Mr Smith.

John cast an eye over the panel and said. 'Don't worry now. We have to blow ballast soon, so we can sort the trim out.' John assured Tug. 'Can we maintain periscope depth?'

'Yes Sir. At the moment yes.'

'Okay. Up periscope.' John commanded. A switch was flicked and a wooshing sound accompanied the glistening silver tube rising quickly upwards in the centre of the control room. The devices control cables flapped around as they were unwound allowing for the rise. John grabbed the hand controls and unfolded them. He rotated his body around whilst he scanned the sea above them. It was a clear day although it was getting late. It was summer time which thankfully helped their situation. He could see nothing of the buoy nor the escaped man. John set the rudder to give a turning circle of 1000m. He would progressively reduce this to a minimum of about 250m and he hoped he would be overtaking the towed buoy just as Robinson Crusoe caught up with his own footprints.

After, about an hour, no visual contact was made. The trim was causing a greater problem, so it was decided to surface the conning tower and dispatch Alwyn and Gilly overboard. They would have to locate the end of the cord and haul in the buoy.

Alwyn and Gilly were in the control room ready to remove the lower conning tower hatch when ordered. Carefully Tug controlled the High-Pressure air to the ballast tanks. Something was wrong with the after ones. A longer time was needed, compared to the front end. However, he managed to bring the submarine to a depth where the pressure hull was still below the waves, but the conning tower was clear. 'Okay sir.' Tug said. Alwyn removed the lower hatch and entered the conning tower followed by Gilly. The upper hatch was opened, and fresh air wafted down into the submarine. Alwyn had prepared a thick rope to dangle over the side to enable him and Gilly to scale the side of the conning tower to get back on board. John followed Alwyn and Gilly, so he could watch their progress. John had briefed them both where to locate the end of the buoy cord. They would have to dive down the side of the pressure hull to locate it. When John got to the top Alwyn was already in the water and Gilly quickly followed.

Tug was concerned with the amount of air used to partially surface the submarine. He knew they would have to run the air compressors, to replenish the air, else they would not be able to surface into the hold of the mother-ship. They would have to run diesels to get the power required by the compressors. This meant, as soon as the buoy was destroyed, and everyone back on board they would have to steam well out of the area because emergency services would be responding to the signal of the 'Submarine Lost' Buoy. One thing in their favour was it was getting dark, so the diesel exhaust could not be seen. At this moment the main motor was stopped, and the submarine was drifting. The missiles required a hovering system to maintain an accurate and stable depth for launching. This system was now being used to maintain the pressure hull beneath the waves, but something was wrong. The back end of the submarine was heavy and getting heavier.

John could see Alwyn had located the tethering cord of the buoy, but he had nowhere to stand to haul the thing in. He ordered Tug to blow main ballast and surface the Submarine. Tug did this, and the front end rose quickly. However, the back end did not. Tug quickly realised two things. The after end of the submarine was too heavy and not all the air was getting into the aft ballast tanks. Submarine Messenger sat in the water with its bow exposed. If anyone would see it, they could see the two large diameter intakes to the JIDs, making the sign of infinity. Two grotesque nostrils fringed with the nozzles for the jet engine exhaust used to form the steam bubble that enabled the Messenger to travel at great speed. John looked aft and could see the tip of the rudder had disappeared. Mr John Smith for the very first time lost his cool. He knew there was something drastically wrong and if the Messenger could not surface it would be safer dived. He knew the average depth was no more than 300 feet and the Messenger could sit comfortable on the sea bed. John still had high hopes of completing his mission. The mother-ship could lift the Messenger from the sea bed into its hold. 'Cut the fucking cord.' he screamed at Alwyn 'Cut the fucking cord.' he commanded again. John realised they were not going to recover it, so the next best option would be to just let it go. The angle of the boat was getting worse. He had to see the line cut before he went below. Alwyn was sawing at it with his divers' knife. The cord had a steel wire core and his knife was useless. He looked up at John desperately. 'Fucking useless cunt!' Mr Smith shouted at him. Mr Smith turned away from him and descended the ladder closing the upper hatch behind him. 'Open fwd. main vents!' He bellowed the order. 'Get as many revs as you can out of that fucking main motor!' John felt the angle of the Messenger change; it was beginning to level out. John jumped down to the control room floor. 'Okay, now open the after vents.' The submarine began to move forwards and level off. Soon the back end began to sag.

'I think the aft escape compartment is flooded.' Tug announced. He didn't ask about Alwyn or Gilly. He knew the answer. John went to the sound room. 'What's the state of the sea bed?' he asked Joe.

Chapter 16.

Recovery

I was staring up at an opaque grey sky when I felt a weight jump on my chest. The blurry face of a dog appeared and disappeared then reappeared again with a steamy tongue flopping out of its mouth. It was a Border Collie and the face had an element of a smile about it. I could hear the muffled sound of the sea and the squawking of seagulls but not much else. I couldn't move anything. I was cold. No, I was freezing cold. The weight lifted as the dog jumped off.

I couldn't remember anything else. It was as if nothing had ever happened in my life. I was just eyes looking up to the sky and the sky was blurry. Then there was another sensation – a sharp pain in my shoulder. Where the dog's face was there was now a face of an old man staring down at me with wide blue eyes. He wore a cap and a white woolly beard hid his cheeks and jaw. The jaw dropped open and the face disappeared. I heard him shout

'Reenie!' I faintly heard him shout again and then I sank back into the blackness the Border Collie had disturbed me from.

When I next opened my eyes, I was looking at a white ceiling. I was in a very bright room. I moved my eyes and realised the opaqueness had gone. My head hurt, and I couldn't move it. I could not move my arms or my legs. I knew I had arms and legs because I could wiggle my fingers and toes. I was no longer cold. At the extreme movements of my eyes I could see white walls. One wall had a white door in it and the wall opposite had a window with white curtains. Through the window I could see a light grey sky that was almost white. I could hear nothing except some faint rustling of paper. It was paper being turned as opposed to paper being screwed up. It was a gently rustling. I closed my eyes and went back into the darkness.

The blackness was all consuming and oppressive. I had no thoughts in my head nor dreams. My life alternated from brief glimpses of the white room to long bouts of blackness. I don't know how long this went on for but one occasion, when I opened my eyes, a lady's face was staring back down at me. She was probably about fifty years old and her face was a welcomed sight for me. She was not the most beautiful lady in the world but far from ugly. It was the face of a grandmother. I desperately tried to concentrate on her presence and not slip back into darkness. 'Hello' she said softly 'are you with us now?' I tried to speak but couldn't. I tried to nod my head, but it would not move. I could feel a stiff collar around it as if I had broken my neck. I blinked my eyes open and shut to try and communicate with her. 'Yes, I believe you are. I'll get the Doctor.' I couldn't stay and went again into darkness.

The next time I opened my eyes there was a man's face next to the lady's in my field of vision. I immediately felt more alert. 'Now, how do you feel?' the man's face asked. My eyes did another scan of the room and an incredible amount of information was sent to my brain. I was in a hospital. I had tubes in my arms and the back of my hands. The tubes went to bottles hanging upside down by my sides. Either side of the bed were machines with flashing, pulsating lights and a small oscilloscope screen drawing the trace of my heart beat. I tried to move my tongue in my mouth, but it was stuck; it was dry and thick. Sensing my problem, the lady offered a tube of a bottle to my mouth and I felt a warm liquid flow. I savoured this and finally swallowed. More came and soon my tongue was free.

'Is that better?' the lady asked.

'Yes.' I croaked finally. I also tried to nod again.

The doctor gently placed his hand upon my forehead indicating I should not try to move my head. He must have seen a worried look on my face. 'Don't worry. Everything will be alright now. You have suffered a fracture to your cranium. We had to put you to sleep for a while.' *Fuck me*! I thought. I had a dog once that I had to have put to sleep and that was pretty permanent. 'We do that in instance such as this whilst the swelling of the brain subsides.' The doctor was younger than the lady whom I now considered must be a nurse. 'Do you know what happened to you?' I thought hard for a while. Some memories were jostling around in my brain, but nothing made sense. I knew I was on a Submarine and had seen a pile of dead bodies. I sort of remember getting out and leaving the door open, so the water could get in. I felt guilty that I had done something terribly wrong. I needed time to think before I said anything. I was sure I was going to be in big trouble.

'No.' I croaked at him.

'What is your name?' he asked. Now, is this a test or what. I had to think but, I did remember my name. I decided not to tell him. If I pretended I had lost my memory, I could not be blamed for anything. At least it would give me time to think and remember more. I tried to shake my head but again he put a preventative hand on my forehead.

'No, no I don't.' the croaking was subsiding as some saliva was beginning to flow lubricating my tongue more.

'Don't worry. That's not uncommon with your injury. Things will start to come back soon.' He went to the foot of the bed and it appeared he was discussing papers with the nurse. 'I'll come back and see you later. The nurse will do some tests.'

The nurse asked a lot of questions about my arms and legs as she manipulated and massaged them. I was beginning to feel more alive. She removed some of the needles in my arm, and with them went some of the bottles. The nurse released the straps around the neck collar and opened the front. 'How does that feel?' she asked, smiling expectantly.

'Good.'

'Try moving you head from side to side. Your neck may be a bit stiff, so it may hurt.'

I did move it and it did hurt but she removed the neck collar totally and I felt a lot better for the freedom.

'Where am I?' I asked her.

'We are in the Queen Elizabeth Hospital in Glasgow. You were found on a beach near Ardnamurchan. West Scotland in the highlands. Came here by helicopter.'

'Oh.' I have no clue where Ardnamurchan is, but I do remember a dog. I decided I would not say anything until I remembered what happened to me.

The next day I was feeling better. I was sitting up in bed and had a bandage around my head. I had eaten breakfast and lunch and drank copious amounts of water and fruit drinks. I even got up and went to the toilet by myself although I was a bit wobbly on my feet. I felt much better.

My memory returned, although I said nothing to the Hospital staff. No one has said anything about the submarine escape suit, the memory module or the bottle of Bells. I don't know if the whisky survived but I do know I was cured of the craving for it. I didn't want McEwans either. I knew I had passed through a life changing experience and alcohol would not play any further part of my future. Having said that it was because of the effect of the alcohol, that I found myself safe in the after-escape compartment when the rest of the crew were being slaughtered. I asked the nurses what I was wearing when I was admitted but she said she did not know and there was nothing in my cupboard. I discovered I had been there for just over two weeks. I asked for the newspapers but there was nothing about a lost or stolen Submarine, and neither any information about it on the TV. I couldn't just ask about it either.

I knew someone would come soon asking me a shit-load of questions, and that would mean they know something. I didn't know if I should tell someone about the murders. I am sure I flooded the after-escape compartment which probably meant the messenger would sink and quite probably the rest of the people on board would have died. That makes me a murderer also. No. Best thing is say nothing. The real best thing is to get out of this hospital. But I couldn't just walk out – I had no clothes.

The next day I felt almost normal. I had undergone a series of physical tests and the doctor declared all my faculties were back to normal. I could read and write, and the wobbliness left my walking. The doctor assured me my memory would return for sure; I still pretended not to remember anything.

During the late afternoon the nurse announced I had a visitor. I didn't know what to expect. She stood aside, and a Mr Gary Osbourne appeared around the door. I could not pretend I didn't know him as I could not conceal my surprise at seeing him. My surprise was also coupled with a rising sense of fear. 'I'll leave you alone.' The nurse said, as she moved around him and closed the door as she left.

'Hello Chief Clark,' Gary said as he approached me with his hand outstretched. 'How are you feeling. You have had a bit of an ordeal.' He pulled up a chair and sat by the bed.

There was not enough time to think. Why is he here? What does he know? 'Hello,' I replied. 'I am feeling fine.' Then added 'Now.'

'Yes. Well. There are some people downstairs who will want to talk to you soon. They will explain everything. I have some good news for you.' I didn't say anything. I just nodded at him. 'You will be pleased to know the police have dropped all charges against you.'

'Good.'

'The police were watching the address you had indicated and, sure enough, Sally turned up. She immediately admitted she was driving the car on the evening when you were apprehended. She told the police she left you there to fix the car because she needed to use the toilet. The garage was shut so she went to the train station. Apparently, she fell asleep. When she woke up, she returned to the car, but it was no longer there. The police had to move it, but she didn't know that. Anyway, she went back to the station to wait for the morning train to Clydebank.'

'Ah. That's good news.'

'When the police quizzed her about the car being stolen, she said she knew nothing about that. Apparently, the car was owned by her daughter's husband. As you know her daughter, and her husband, have separated. The daughter considered the car also belonged to her so took it. Sally used the car thinking indeed, it belonged to her daughter. It was considered a domestic issue and the husband didn't want to press any charges.'

'Ok. That is good news. Thanks for letting me know.'

'Furthermore, the police could not charge Sally with anything. There was no accident, so she did not flee the scene and it was too late to breathalyse her. The police suspected she had also been drinking heavily.'

'So, what happened to the car?'

'The police had to get a tow truck to remove it and it was taken to a compound. Sally refused to collect it, so the husband went. He had to pay for the tow truck and storage. The amount of money requested was significant and the husband said the car was not worth it so just left it.'

I was really pleased to know everything turn out well with this. However, it paled into insignificance considering the events that took place afterwards.

'Now, Chief Clark,' Gary stood, 'I'll let the Admiral know you are ready.' Then he let himself out the door.

Admiral! Shit! Now it's getting serious.

The nurse pushed the door open again and stood aside. 'More visitors,' she said.

FOSM entered and I was really pleased to see him. At least it was someone whom I had met before and who had treated me well. He wore civilian clothes and looked every bit a successful business man. He was followed by two more suit wielding smart men. 'I'll get some more chairs.' The nurse fussed.

'Hello Chief Clark.' He said offering his hand of friendship. 'I trust you have recovered well from your ordeal,' I didn't reply other than responding to his 'Hello'. 'This gentleman here.' Indicating the man by his side 'Is Stuart Gibson. He works for the British secret service.' Stuart was tall, not as tall as the Admiral, and he was equally smart. I guessed he would be about my age. 'This other gentleman is Henry Heinricht. He works for the American secret service.' Henry was older and shorter. His hair was thinning and receding, but his eyes were as sharp as lasers.

By this time, they all had seats, so they lowered themselves into them.

'They tell me you have lost your memory, but Mr Osbourne says it's not so.' I felt embarrassed and fidgeted my hands in my lap. 'Now, first-of-all chief, I don't want you to worry that I have come to see you with these gentlemen. We need to know a few things from you.' I looked up at him with a certain amount of relief. 'And I'm sure you need to know a few things.' I nodded. 'Well, you were found on Ardnamurchan beach and thought to be dead. The harbour master was called, and he collected you in his land-rover. When he got you to his office, they cut open the escape suit and discovered you were still alive. You were transferred here with a broken skull and, it seems, no other injuries. You arrived here with only your overalls. The escape suit and the other stuff remained with the Harbour Master. No one knew what the escape suit was as they had never seen anything like it before. After a few days it was identified as a Submarine Escape suit and the Admiralty was informed and they took charge of it along with your bottle of whisky, water bottles, ships biscuits and the memory cassette.' He paused and watched my face as he mentioned the memory cassette. I struggled hard to meet his eyes without showing any emotion or guilt. 'I will ask you more about how you came by this cassette later. As far as I understood, only I knew of the existence of the recording system on board; myself, these gentlemen and their departments.' He indicated his colleagues. 'We examined the contents of the cassette and it revealed a ghastly story. I suspect you know the story.'

'Well, I know what I saw and heard,'

'Okay. I won't ask you to recount it all, but we are interested to know how you knew about the TELSA equipment room?' I anticipated this question and I was determined I would not tell them anything about Jake. I hoped Jake trusted me enough when I promised him I would say nothing, so whenever he should be questioned, he too, can say he was not involved.

'Well, Sir I was making myself familiar with the submarine, I needed to know everything about it and where everything was. It was my responsible duty to do that. I had seen the stores rack, in the escape compartment, with the TELSA cabinet adjoining it. Some things seemed odd about them. I couldn't understand why these TELSA cabinets should be installed away from the main cabinets above the main engines. The cabinets, in the after-escape compartment, were only thin and so would not occupy too much room if installed with the others. The front of the stores racks, behind the mesh door, were all small – only a couple of inches tall. I didn't know how far they went back. If they went all the way, then they would be ridiculously long. As the stores racks were so thin, then it must mean they hold very small components. Electronic components are small as are seals for valves etcetera. I am sorry sir, but it didn't make sense. I looked, in the ship's and stores books but no information was available; it's as if they didn't exist. I wanted to investigate but didn't want to do any damage, so I took the lynch pins out of the hinges and discovered the stores fronts were just dummies and all connected to make a door.' All three were leaning forwards, looking intensely at me. 'I was able to open the door and, well, you know what I found.'

'So how did you know about the memory cassettes? What compelled you to take one with you.' Stuart asked me. I was thinking whilst I formulated my reply. It seemed Stuart was trying to catch me out although there was only inquisitiveness showing on his face.

'Sir,' I addressed him respectfully, 'I soon realised cameras were placed all over the submarine and there was a facility to look back on events that had happened previously. For this to happen the information must be stored somewhere and I assumed that place would be the cassettes. I didn't remove them for inspection as I didn't want to disturb the system. One was marked 'Master' the other 'Duplicate.' When I left, I extracted the 'Duplicate' and considered the 'Master' would continue recording until the water level rose and, would probably, destroy the system.'

'Okay,' Stuart said and seemed satisfied with my reply.

The Admiral spoke again. 'Well done Chief. You should have been a detective.' I was pleased they all seemed to accept my explanation and Jake would be safe. 'Now just before you escaped you released the 'Submarine Lost' buoy. You would then know that the signal would be detected, before too long, and rescue services would be on their way.'

'Yes Sir.'

'So why escape? Why not wait until you were rescued?'

'Firstly, I was not 100% confident the Buoy would work and, secondly if it did, would the rescue services arrive before the mother-ship came and took us away?

'So, you deliberately left off the vent cap when you escaped?' Now there seemed an accusing tone in the Admirals voice. If I said I just forgot, then I could not be accused of deliberately sinking the Submarine. But, I did deliberately leave it off! I did it to save the submarine from being stolen. 'We now know you did this deliberately because you just told us you considered the 'Master' cassette would continue to function until the water level rose and destroyed the equipment.'

'Believe me sir I considered it very carefully. If I were just to leave, then there was a chance the mother-ship would arrive before the rescue services. A flooded escape compartment would not destroy the submarine. I considered it would cause it to be in a situation where it could not surface so the safest thing would be to sit it on the bottom of the sea. I also considered we were still on the European continental shelf and thought the depth was no greater than 300 feet. So yes, I deliberately left the vent cap off Sir,'

'After you left the submarine partially surfaced and two men exited the conning tower in an endeavour to recover the buoy and disarm it. By this time the stern was getting heavy and causing problems. Mr Smith tried to surface but could not. The Messenger reached a dangerous angle and Mr Smith ordered the venting of the forward ballast tanks and so diving the submarine. The two men were abandoned on the surface. The Submarine did safely settle on the sea bed.'

'Who was left on the surface sir?'

'Chief Petty Officer Leonard and Leading Hand Thomas Gill. They both perished and ended up washed up on a beach close to where you were found.' I was filled with mixed emotions now. Immediately I felt sad for Lanky, but the sadness was soon replaced with a feeling that justice had been done. I also thought of his boat. His dream just sitting there in all its splendour and half a million quid in cash on board. I never knew what Gilly would do with his bounty but, again it would be a dream dashed with cash in suspension. I was beginning to feel a depression creeping over me. The vision of a pile of bodies in the torpedo compartment with Jock dragging them off one by one. A great sadness overwhelmed me. A shivering went down my spine and I could feel goose pimples tingling on my arm. Tears filled my eyes and I could not help sobbing like a baby. I was wailing in grief. Since that vision, this is the first time I have thought of it, and it was me weeping for all their mother's. I was grieving for their children.

Their ex wives may rejoice but they would not if they had seen their former loved ones being dragged from a heap of death to be unceremoniously dumped in a tank and then devoured by concentrated sulphuric acid and finally flushed into the sea as some noxious liquid mixture. The power of my sobs hurt my stomach. I felt a warm soft hand on my shoulder. I tried desperately to bring myself under control. My hands were clutched over my face as I tried to control my breathing. My hands were soaked with my tears and I could taste the saltiness leaking into my mouth. I finally raised my head and dried my face with one of the bed sheets.
'I am sorry about that sir.' The hand was patting my shoulder now. 'Don't know what came over me.'

'Don't worry Clark. I too could not control myself when I saw the images recorded by the cassette.' I don't know if he was just trying to console me. I looked up and the other two gentlemen had left the room. 'Chief, you will be pleased to know we were able to recover the Messenger.' I looked up in surprise and was genuinely pleased. We found it on the sea bed in 180 feet of water. The remaining crew were still on board and agreed to assist with the recovery. They accepted the game was up and they were caught. When we arrived, there was a large super-tanker in the area, but it soon vanished. We did not know the reason why it was there, and we didn't pay it any attention. In fact, we were pleased when it disappeared. We were able to bring the Messenger to the surface with flotation devices. Divers entered the after-escape tower and with submersible pumps, the after-escape compartment was pumped out. The Messenger was towed to the Holy Loch and actually, suffered next to no damage. Your decision, to leave off the vent cap, was the correct one. We applaud you for your actions and consider, that because of them, we still have our newest Submarine. It will be renamed and brought back into service.

I had recovered my composure somewhat and digested all I had been informed of. 'So, I am not in the shit then sir?' I asked.

'No Clark. You are not in the shit. You are a fucking hero.'

Now normally the story would end here but there are some loose ends to tie up. The Admiral continued. 'In this instance the Navy does not want heroes. If we celebrate heroes, then we must admit there was a mutiny on board and our Submarine was nearly stolen. I hope you can understand, this would not be a good image.' I could see that. 'CPO Leonard and Leading Hand Gill were discovered in their wet-suits with no names and no insignia. They have been categorised as 'Unknown'. Their bodies fell victim to hungry fish and birds as well as the ill effects of being in the sea for about five days. Their facial features do not resemble their ID photograph.' The Admiral could see the distaste on my face. 'The remaining seven crew, from the Messenger, are in solitary confinement. They will remain in solitary confinement for the rest of their lives. They will never go to court or anywhere else.'

The Admiral leant back in his seat with his hands on his knees. 'So, you are the only surviving member of Submarine Messenger. The only person who was on board and knows what really happened.' The Admiral was looking intently at me again, with no flicker of emotion on his face. I had no idea what his thoughts were. I don't know if I should be afraid or not. 'At the moment there is no information about this incident in the public domain. The organisation that assisted us, a Dutch company, with the recovery of the Submarine believed they were assisting us with an escape exercise involving another submarine. No one is expecting to hear from messenger for another couple of months or so. The signal from the 'Submarine Lost' buoy was officially reported as 'Spurious'. You.' The Admiral nodded his head towards me, 'could be an embarrassment to us if we returned you to Faslane.'

'No Sir, I'll say nothing. I promise.' I blurted like a small child might.

'You see, what can happen is that Messenger will not come back from patrol and, after some investigation, can be described as lost. The Navy can name the lost crew and pay the appropriate compensation and pensions as normal, and a memorial ceremony would follow. Your name could be on that list and payments would be received by your ex-wives.' Shit! I'm going to disappear. 'We can give you a new identity. You could receive a new Passport and driving license – you would no longer be banned. We will continue to pay you your Naval salary up until you reach the age of 40 years and then we will pay your pension. Additionally, we will Pay a severance amount of £100,000 with the understanding that this will finance a new house for you where-ever you decide to live. A full set of service records would be produced along with qualifications and discharge documents in your new name. Because you have no children, I feel this could be a very acceptable solution for everyone. How does that sound?'

'It's a lot to take in sir but I guess I don't have a choice.'

'If you do not like this option, I can guarantee you will not like the alternative. We just want you to leave this hospital bed and assume your new life. Don't mention your experiences to anyone. The two gentlemen, who were here earlier, represent the highest level of authority available with regards to getting things done. Someone spouting off a bizarre story of a plot to steal a submarine could easily be classified as insane.' He paused to let me digest this. 'And we all know what can happen to insane people.' I acknowledged the veiled threat.

'You say I will assume my new identity when I leave here?'

'Yes.'

'In a couple of days? That quick?'

'Yes. The doctors say you are fit enough. You have to be careful with your head – no contact sports.' Now the Admiral was smiling. 'I assume you agree?' I nodded. 'Well someone will return here in two days with details of a new bank account. You will have a current account into which your salary will be paid, and a savings account into which the severance pay will be deposited. You will be given a file of all the new documents. Additionally, we can bring your clothes from your inboard cabin. You will also be entitled to a Railway warrant to any station in the UK.'

'Okay sir. It seems you have everything covered. I am impressed.' The Admiral stood up smiling and extended his hand again. I took it and returned his squeeze. 'Sir?' I asked. 'How is Chief Baldwin. I know I will never see him again but would like to know if he is okay.'

'He is okay and should make a full recovery.' As an afterthought he added 'He will consider himself the luckiest man in the Navy when he hears Submarine Messenger has been lost.'

'Yes, he will.' I was pleased to know there would be no lasting ill effects of his broken legs.

The Admiral paused at the door 'Oh,' He said, as an afterthought, 'I need to know what new name you would like and where the train ticket needs to be for.'

I thought for only a moment. 'I'd like to be known as Owen Jones and I want to go to Poole.'

Three days later I arrived at the offices of Princes Boat Storage and entered through the main door. A service hatch presented it to me and soon it was slid upwards and a cheerful elderly man poked his shiny head through it. 'Yes.' He said. 'Can I help you?' Well, here we go.

'I have come to collect me boat.' I told him.

'Name?'

'Owen Jones.'

'You have some form of identification?

'Yes.' I placed my new passport and driving license before him. He shuffled some papers and then looked up at me.

'You didn't have identification before. You didn't present identification when you ordered the boat.'

'No, I didn't. But I am presenting it now.'

'Well, I need the secret code you gave.'

'But I've got these.' I was shaking the documents in front of his nose.

'I need the secret code Mr Jones.'

I remembered the conversation when Alwyn was telling Dennis about this secret code. He told him he was on Valiant and, at that time, the senior rates mess were drinking more beer than the aircraft carrier Ark Royal. He said he would never forget his bar number. Well, I was also on board Valiant, at that time, and it is true, we were ordering more beer than Ark Royal. I was beer caterer so had to account for all this beer and present everyone with their bar bills, so they could pay for it. I knew everyone's bar number.

'Yes, of course. It's AL29.'

'Thank you, Mr Jones,' He shuffled some more paper then told me. 'Go through that door and I'll see you the other side. I met him outside.

'Just follow me and I'll take you to your boat.' I followed behind.

‘Do you have a name for your boat yet Mr Jones?’ he asked casually over his shoulder.

‘Yes. I think I will call it Messenger.’

ABOUT THE AUTHOR

Christopher P Clark was brought up in a small village in the fens of England, badly educated and destined for a life of crime. He joined the Royal Navy where he had a second chance of education. He served 17 years, mostly in the submarine service. On leaving the Navy he was employed by a company selling lighthouse equipment. He traveled the World installing new equipments and converting old systems to solar power. Chris then joined the printing industry followed by the packaging industry. In the early nineties he started his own business. He went bust twice and then got the formula right and made some money. He was married twice, divorced twice and lost all his money twice. In 2007, aged 56, he packed all his possessions into the back of a motor-home and moved to Spain. Chris built his own house, single-handed, where he now lives with his new beautiful wife from Colombia. He still thinks he has many more stories to tell.

Printed in Great Britain
by Amazon